"Sorry," he said. "Couldn't resist."

"You couldn't resist dunking me?"

Aaron's smile faded a little. His dark eyes locked with hers. "I couldn't resist putting my hands on you."

"Oh." Had the water suddenly gotten hotter? Shelby felt a definite wave of heat course through her, and was almost surprised that steam didn't rise from her skin. "Um—"

"No one's watching," he murmured, reaching out to draw her closer with his left arm around her waist. He braced his other arm on her watercraft to support them. "I'm not playing a part. So if you want me to back off, just give me a shove."

She put a hand on his shoulder, but only to steady herself in the water. She had no intention of pushing him away.

Dear Reader,

For me, revisiting characters from previous books is like
catching up with old friends. I love to sit down with a cup
of tea and find out what's been happening in their lives—
and then to give them new adventures and romance to
entertain my readers. Members of the Walker family I
introduced in my long-running Family Found series,
twins Aaron and Andrew Walker first appeared as adults
in *The Texan's Tennessee Romance*. They were so amused
by their cousin Casey's romance that I figured they
deserved to be blindsided by Cupid, themselves!

Aaron Walker is startled by a big hug from a pretty blonde
who thinks she is greeting his identical twin, Andrew.
Shelby Bell—a member of the big, close family that owns
and operates the Bell Resort and Marina in southeastern
Texas—is embarrassed by her mistake. Shelby is in
trouble and she had hoped for help from Andrew. Now
Aaron has to convince her that he's the right twin for
the job…and for her. I hope you enjoy their adventures
together. Watch for Andrew's story, *The Texan's Surprise
Baby,* in May 2013.

Gina Wilkins

THE RIGHT TWIN

GINA WILKINS

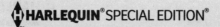 HARLEQUIN® SPECIAL EDITION®

Recycling programs
for this product may
not exist in your area.

ISBN-13: 978-0-373-65730-8

THE RIGHT TWIN

Copyright © 2013 by Gina Wilkins

Printed in U.S.A.

Books by Gina Wilkins

GINA WILKINS

is a bestselling and award-winning author who has written more than seventy novels for Harlequin Books. She credits her successful career in romance to her long, happy marriage and her three "extraordinary" children.

A lifelong resident of central Arkansas, Ms. Wilkins sold her first book to Harlequin in 1987 and has been writing full-time since. She has appeared on the Waldenbooks, B. Dalton and *USA TODAY* bestseller lists. She is a three-time recipient of a Maggie Award for Excellence, sponsored by Georgia Romance Writers, and has won several awards from the reviewers of *RT Book Reviews*.

For my friends on Facebook
who engage in such interesting discussions with me.
"Like" my Facebook author page to join us!

Chapter One

Just once, Aaron Walker thought with a deep sigh, it would be nice if his twin brother, Andrew, would be the one to screw up. Nothing major, just something embarrassing or a little reckless. Something that would get their large, loving and well-intended family in a tizzy about anything other than Aaron's latest debacle. But even as the selfish wish crossed his mind, he knew it was futile. Andrew rarely made mistakes, and never of the same magnitude as Aaron's. Andrew was the one more likely to rush to the rescue than to need rescuing.

Sure, Andrew had been known to raise a little hell in his time, especially as a member of the "terrible trio"— the affectionate nickname given to the twins and their same-age cousin, Casey Walker, during their mischief-prone childhood and teen years. But now Casey had settled down with a wife and a legal practice in east Tennessee, while Andrew was rising in the ranks of the family-owned investigation and security business. Aaron was the only one still regularly causing general concern and disapproval.

Especially during the past few months, all Andrew did was work and complain about Aaron's lack of focus. Aaron had just endured another one of those brotherly lectures, triggered by his decision to quit yet another job that hadn't been working out for him. Andrew had stated that it was time for thirty-year-old Aaron to get serious about his life and his future. If he was determined not to work in the family business, he needed to find a purpose, and soon. Andrew wasn't the first family member who'd given Aaron that speech—he'd also heard it from his dad, his uncles, his mother, his grandfather and a couple of random cousins—but Andrew was the one who most annoyed him. Had Andrew not been called out of his office for a quick consultation, they'd probably be in the middle of a heated quarrel right this minute.

Though Andrew had asked him to wait, Aaron decided to make his escape, postponing the quarrel for later. Just as he rose to walk out of the office, a colorful brochure lying on the floor beside the trash can caught his eye. It looked as though Andrew had tossed it that way and missed the receptacle. For no particular reason, Aaron picked it up and studied the bright photographs printed on the glossy trifold.

Bell Resort and Marina was located on Lake Livingston, a large reservoir roughly a hundred and seventy-five miles southeast of Dallas. Aaron had never been to that particular resort, but he'd visited the lake a time or two. Good fishing, peaceful setting, nice scenery. Eyeing the photos of people skiing, swimming, picnicking and lounging in the sun, he wished he were there rather than here in Dallas with his beloved but disapproving family. Just for a little while, until he could return to them with a solid new career plan in mind. All he needed was a little time to think, to regroup, to determine why he seemed to be the only one in his overachieving family who hadn't yet found the path he wanted to follow. On impulse, he stuffed the brochure in his pocket and headed for the door.

Twenty-four hours later, he stood beside his car, idly watching numbers flash past on the gas pump from which he was filling his tank. It was midafternoon on this second Tuesday in June, the temperature hovering at ninety degrees even though summer was barely underway. The heavy scent of gasoline hung in the overheated air. He reached up to tug at the neckline of the bright blue T-shirt he wore with khaki cargo shorts and sandals. His longish, near-black hair clung damply to the back of his neck. After his almost four-hour drive, he looked forward to sitting under a tree by the water's edge with a cold beer.

According to his directions, Bell Resort was only another fifteen-minute drive away from this little town where he'd stopped for a fuel-and-restroom break. There wasn't much to see here—from where he stood, he spotted a few houses, a thrift shop, a dollar store and a tiny post office. Just the sort of laid-back area he needed in which to brood for a few days. Maybe a week. There was no one here to shake a head or a finger at him, no one to lecture him or advise him, no one here who knew him at all....

Even as that thought crossed his mind, a young woman in a tank top and shorts squealed and almost tackled him with a hug. "You're back! It's so good to see you again!"

Aaron staggered a little with the assault, but quickly recovered his balance. He couldn't say he was displeased about suddenly finding his arms filled with a petite, curvy blonde, but he had no clue who she was. "Um—"

She drew back a few inches to smile up at him and for a moment he forgot how to form words. Damn, but she was pretty. Clear blue eyes framed in long, dark lashes. Dimples deep enough to fall into. A nose that could only be described as "pert," and full lips curved into a smile that made his knees feel suddenly shaky. Her scoop-necked top revealed the upper curves of perfectly sized, creamy breasts, and he could tell by feel that the rest of her was just as nicely formed.

Oh, yeah, coming here had definitely been a good idea.

"You are coming to Bell Resort, right?" she asked, surprising him again. "You're here because I sent you the brochure and the reminder that you're always welcome?"

The Bell Resort and Marina had been Aaron's destination, though he hadn't taken the time to make reservations. It looked ideal in the brochure his brother had tossed in the trash, but Aaron figured he'd find a room somewhere else on the lake if the resort was full. He hadn't seen the personal invitation that had been enclosed with the brochure, so either Andrew had held on to it or thrown it away separately. "Well, yes, I thought I'd relax for a few days if there's a vacancy. But—"

"Great!" She hugged him again, then pulled away. He released her reluctantly. "Of course there's a vacancy for you! Everyone is going to be so happy to see you. We're all still so grateful to you for what you did for us last year."

"Listen, you—"

"You've grown out your hair," she said, studying him with her head cocked to one side. "I like it."

He was beginning to understand. Now if only he could get a few words in to explain it to her. "Thanks, but I—"

"You should see Lori's hair. She dyed it coal-black with blue streaks. Dad nearly had a conniption. Pop said she looks like she bruised her head. Steven thinks it's funny, but Lori complains that he's laughing at her. Mom and Mimi just sigh a lot."

"Yes, well, I—"

"Hey, Shelby, how's it going?" a lanky young man in a faded camo T-shirt, denim shorts and a sweat-stained red ball cap called out as he ambled from the store toward a battered pickup truck parked at one of the other gas pumps.

"I'm good, Bubba," the blonde replied. "Look who's back."

The guy nodded. "Yo, Mr. Walker. 'Sup?"

Resigned, Aaron nodded in return, saying, "Hey," an all-purpose greeting that seemed to satisfy the younger man.

Shelby turned back to Aaron when Bubba drove off. Her bright smile faded when she asked, "Does Hannah know you're here? She's out of town for a few weeks, visiting her mom's family near Shreveport. I doubt she'll be back while you're here."

"No one knows I'm here," he said with a shrug. "It was an impulsive trip."

She laughed and patted his arm, her momentary gravity evaporating. She was definitely the demonstrative type—not that he was complaining. "That's so funny. I never would have pegged you as impulsive, but I'm glad you're here, anyway."

He nodded, wryly amused now that he'd finally figured out what was going on. He tightened the gas cap on his car and closed the flap, having already paid by credit card. Even here it seemed he was living in his brother's shadow.

"Listen, before we head for the resort, would you mind if I buy you a soda or a cup of coffee inside?" Shelby asked, gazing up at him with a thoughtful expression. "There's something I'd like to discuss with you before you see everyone else. Something's been bothering me and everyone thinks I'm being overly dramatic, but maybe while you're here you could help me out a little? You know, tell me if there's reason for me to be concerned or if I really am nuts?"

He didn't have the faintest idea what she'd just asked, but something about the way she looked at him made him want to agree to any request she made of him. "Let me move my car away from the pump and I'll meet you inside," he said.

The return of her generous smile rewarded him. "Thank you. I knew you would help. See you inside."

He watched as she turned and all but sprinted for the door of the station, her shoulder-length blond curls bouncing against her shoulders. The back side of her was every bit as appealing as the front, he thought, his gaze lingering on those snug shorts. Making himself look away, he climbed into his car. He would park and then join Shelby inside. Maybe when she finally ran out of steam he would find a chance to break it to her that she had embraced the wrong twin.

There was something different about Andrew Walker, but Shelby Bell couldn't quite put a finger on what it was. It wasn't just his hair, though he'd worn it almost militarily short when she'd met him last year. The color of strong, rich coffee, it looked much softer now that he'd let it grow. A girl's fingers could get lost in there for a while. His eyes were the same deep brown she remembered, and his facial structure was classically handsome. But something had changed....

She'd met Andrew almost a year ago when he'd spent nearly two weeks at the resort, helping her family with a sensitive legal matter. Her dad and grandfather had hired the private investigator from a Dallas firm, and Andrew had pretty much single-handedly saved the family business from a spiteful con man. By the time he'd left, he'd been the family hero, invited to return for free lodging whenever he needed a vacation from his demanding job.

Like the rest of the family, Shelby had been extremely grateful to Andrew for what he'd done for them. She had liked him very much, and she'd certainly noticed how good-looking he was, but there had been no romantic chemistry between them. She had spent little time alone with him, always surrounded by family and guests of the resort. And she'd been dating Pete then, so she hadn't really thought of Andrew in that way. Nor had he seemed particularly interested in her other than as a member of the family he had worked for and befriended.

She couldn't quite figure out what had changed, why she was suddenly noticing things like the shallow indention in his chin and the way his T-shirt outlined the hard, lean body beneath. Why her toes were curling in her flip-flops just because of the way he smiled at her from across the table. She didn't remember him smiling quite like that before. Maybe it had been too long since she'd been alone with an attractive man. She'd broken up with Pete last winter—well, okay, Pete had dumped her, but it sounded better her way—and she had been too busy to even go on a date since.

Drawing her thoughts from such an irrelevant path, she started talking as soon as they were seated in a small snack corner of the station with their drinks— iced tea for him, a frozen cherry-flavored drink for her. Now she needed to quickly outline what she wanted to ask him before he had a chance to dismiss her concerns without hearing her out, as her family was prone to do.

"So, I know you've just gotten here and you're probably hoping for a nice, relaxing vacation," she began in a rush of words. "And I know it's presumptuous of me to ask a favor before you even get to the resort, especially after all you did for my family last summer—and even more especially since I can't afford to hire you, exactly. But what I ask would only take a few minutes, and I'll make sure you have a great time at the resort in return. Well, not that I wouldn't do that, anyway—I mean, we all invited you to come back anytime and to make use of all our facilities for a nice, relaxing vacation, which we all figured you needed because you work so hard."

"Shelby—"

She was making such a mess of this. In frustration, she powered on. "There's this guy who's been staying at the resort. He's quiet, doesn't make any trouble, is all paid up, even tips very well. But I don't trust him. There's something hinky going on with him, and no one in the family will listen to me when I try to tell them. You know how they are—'Oh, you're just being Shelby again,' they say. And, okay, I know I get carried away sometimes and maybe overreact a little, but wasn't I the one who just knew the evil ex had been stealing from us last year? I kept saying that if we looked hard enough, we'd find plenty of ammunition against him and his stupid, greedy lawsuits, and I was right, wasn't I?"

"Okay." He took a sip of his iced tea, and she had a sneaking suspicion that he was trying not to grin. "Why don't you finish telling me about this 'hinky' guy, and then I'll talk?"

She didn't know what it was about her that made people not take her seriously. Just because she was energetic and enthusiastic, quick to show her feelings, a little too prone to jump to conclusions, everyone seemed to think they should just brush off her suggestions and ideas. But Andrew had listened to her last year when she insisted her cousin Hannah's ex-husband had been stealthily stealing from the family business, and that he had then falsified legal claims against them that could have put the resort in serious financial straits had he won. She had even helped Andrew come up with a plan to prove her suspicions, though she had suggested perhaps a half-dozen schemes before she'd stumbled onto one he'd approved. She hoped he would be inclined to listen to her again now.

"So, this guy—he says his name is Terrence Landon, but he doesn't really look like a Terrence, you know? Anyway, he's been at the resort for about two weeks. He pays in cash. Says he's on an extended vacation from a high-stress marketing job in Austin that almost put him in the hospital with high blood pressure and ulcers. Every other day or so, he has men join him—associates, he calls them—for fishing and business talks. They always bring stuff in boxes and cases, and they never seem to leave with the same stuff they brought. And either they're the world's worst fishermen or they just don't try very hard, but they hardly ever bring in a good catch."

"And you think he's—what? Dealing drugs? Weapons?"

She narrowed her eyes on his face, but he didn't seem to be mocking her. It sounded like a legitimate question.

"Maybe," she said cautiously. "Or maybe he's just baking brownies for their kids. Who knows? Dad and Steven both say I'm misinterpreting things and Dad told me to stay away from the guy before I run off a good-paying customer with my 'crazy imagination,' to quote him. Maggie thinks I got a little too enthusiastic about all the private investigating last summer and I'm looking for a way to relive that excitement. As if I'd want to relive that horrible time," she added indignantly. "Poor Hannah still hasn't gotten over the stress and humiliation, which is probably how she ended up…"

She swallowed and shook her head, deciding to focus on one mystery at a time. "Anyway, I'm willing to concede that there's nothing at all suspicious going on with Terrence Landon, but since you're going to be with us for a few days, and since you're trained to look for things like that, maybe if you just happen to bump into him while you're here? Talk with him for a couple minutes or sort of discreetly observe one of his meetings with his associates? Then you can tell me if I'm seeing things that aren't there, or if there really is any reason for me to worry about him staying at the resort."

He had set down his paper cup of iced tea and laced his fingers on the table, looking at her more seriously now.

She swallowed hard in response to his expression. "I'm sorry, was I out of line asking? I know you said you're here for a vacation, and I certainly didn't mean to ruin it for you before you've even unpacked your car. Forget I asked, okay? It's probably nothing. I'll keep an eye on the guy just in case, but you should just relax and have a good time."

He was shaking his head before she finished apologizing. "It isn't that, Shelby. What you asked sounded perfectly reasonable—if I was who you think I am."

She felt a quick jolt of pleasure at having her concerns called *reasonable,* something she'd yet to hear from her family—but then the rest of his words sank in. "I don't understand."

"You see, the thing is, you've made a mistake. I'm not Andrew Walker."

Chapter Two

Aaron's head was spinning a little—both from confusion at trying to follow Shelby's convoluted request and from a growing fascination with her. He liked the way she looked, but he was even more intrigued by the way her mind worked. She was different from the women he'd spent time with lately—and that was a good thing.

He had been almost tempted to allow Shelby to continue believing he was Andrew, just to see how long he could get away with it. It wouldn't be the first time he and his brother had switched places for one reason or another, though it had been years since they'd pulled such a stunt. But then he'd realized he wanted those generous smiles of hers aimed at him, not Andrew, and he'd known it was time to tell her the truth.

"I'm Aaron," he said gently. "Andrew's brother."

She blinked rapidly, her long lashes sweeping her pinkening cheeks. "Twins?"

"Identical," he said, though she'd probably already figured that out. "Though we're told it doesn't run in families, our dad is an identical twin, too. Coincidence, I suppose, but here we are."

"Wow." Her face had turned as cherry-red as her icy drink. "It never even occurred to me—"

"I take it Andrew didn't mention he has a twin?"

She shook her head slowly. "No, but then he didn't talk about himself that much. He was here on a job, after all, though we all got very friendly with him. You're *Aaron?*"

He nodded, familiar with the reaction of new acquaintances shocked by how much he and Andrew looked alike. If it wasn't for their different hair and clothing styles—he favored a more casual and colorful look than his brother—few people outside their family would be able to tell them apart.

She covered her cheeks with her hands. "Oh, my gosh. You must have thought I was crazy when I threw my arms around you out there."

He chuckled. "Actually, I thought I'd just gotten very lucky."

She didn't even seem to catch the joke. She was still shaking her head and looking embarrassed. "And I didn't give you a chance to correct me, did I?"

"Well, no, you—"

"I just kept talking and talking and then I practically dragged you in here to hit you up for a favor."

"Shelby, it's—"

"My family is right. I do get carried away," she muttered in self-recrimination. "I really do need to—"

"Shelby." This time it was he who interrupted, reaching across the table to catch her hands in his just to make sure he had her attention. "My turn to talk, remember?"

She nodded, her slender throat working with the words she must be swallowing.

He squeezed her fingers, then rather reluctantly released her. "I don't think you're crazy. You certainly aren't the first person to mistake me for my brother and you won't be the last. And you didn't have to drag me in here. I'm pleased to have met you."

Her bright blue eyes widened, her humor returning as her blush faded. "Oh, my gosh, we haven't actually met, have we? I'm Shelby. Shelby Bell. It's very nice to meet you, Aaron."

"Bell as in Bell Resort and Marina?"

She nodded. "My paternal great-grandfather built a little bait shop on the river back in the early 1940s. They owned some land on what would become the banks of Lake Livingston when the river was dammed to form a reservoir in the late sixties. My grandfather started Bell Resort with a small marina, bait shop and a few campsites in 1970, and now it's a family-run business. My grandparents have two sons—my dad, Carl Jr., and my uncle, Bryan. Both sons and their wives work in the resort. My brother, Steven, and I have jobs there, along with our cousins, Hannah and Maggie. My youngest sister, Lori, is still in college. She hasn't decided yet if she's going into the family resort or if she wants to do something else. Our parents and grandparents always say they want the kids to follow their own dreams, do whatever they want, but there's still a lot of pressure to stick with the family and keep the resort running. I think poor Steven feels that obligation the most."

Aaron couldn't help wincing a little. "I'm familiar with family pressure."

"Oh, right. The D'Alessandro-Walker Agency. That's how we met Andrew, of course. My cousin's evil ex-husband, Wade Cavender, had been embezzling from the resort for a couple years, and then the bastard had the nerve to try to sue us for a ton of settlement money he wasn't due—extortion, really—and Andrew helped us find proof it was all a scam. He turned over evidence of the embezzlement to the police, which is why Wade is currently in jail, which is exactly where he deserves to be. His sentence wasn't nearly long enough, but I don't think he'll mess with us again when he gets out."

She'd given him a lot of information to process at once. "Um—"

She shook her head quickly. "But maybe you know all that, since I'm sure the case is on file at the D'Alessandro-Walker Agency. It's a family-run business, too, right?"

Since she'd given him the history of her family business, he figured he owed her the same. "The agency was founded by my uncle Tony D'Alessandro, who took on my dad and his twin as partners in the business before I was even born. Several of my cousins, as well as my brother, work for the agency."

Her brows drew downward in what might have been a slight frown of disappointment. "You're not an investigator?"

Now was the time when he should tell her that not only was he not a dashing P.I. like the twin she and her family seemed to idolize, but he was currently unemployed. Again. He cleared his throat. "Like you, I grew up in the family business."

It wasn't exactly a lie. He'd worked in the offices of Dee-Dub, as the agency was familiarly known within the family, during his teen years, breaking away after high school to pursue his own goals. It just happened that none of his experiments had led yet to a career in which he wanted to spend the foreseeable future. He knew it wasn't the investigation and security field.

Shelby's face lit up again and he was selfishly glad he'd prevaricated. "So maybe while you're staying with us, you could still take a look at Terrence Landon?" she asked hopefully. "You know, just to sort of get an impression of whether he's as shady as I think he is?"

He couldn't stand to see disappointment on her face a second time, especially when he knew what Andrew would do in his shoes. "I'm not promising anything, but I guess I could take a discreet look at the guy while I'm here. That doesn't mean I'll agree with your suspicions. Or that I'll even see enough to form a proper opinion of my own."

She waved off his warnings with one hand. "Of course," she said. "Maybe there's nothing to it at all. But I'd feel better if at least someone took me seriously enough to just get a good look at the guy."

Aaron leaned back in his plastic chair and studied her thoughtfully. If he was reading her correctly, this was something else they seemed to have in common. Being the family oddballs, the ones over whom all the others shook their heads and clucked their tongues. Even as he wondered what he was getting himself into, he shrugged. "Sure. I'll check him out."

This time she was the one who reached across the table. She caught both his hands in hers and squeezed. "Thank you, Aaron."

Oh, man. He could be in big trouble, he thought with a hard swallow. Something told him Andrew was not going to like this at all. As for Shelby—would she still look at him with such glowing eyes when she found out that he'd just promised something he was in no way qualified to deliver?

And speaking of his brother, just how had Shelby gazed at *him?*

"Um, you and Andrew…"

She seemed to follow his line of thought easily enough. She laughed again, and every cell in his body responded to the sound. "Me and Andrew? No way. I liked him, of course—the whole family liked him. But as for the two of us—just no sparks, you know?"

Watching her gather their empty cups to toss into the waste can, Aaron wondered if she would say the same thing about him in a few days. As for himself, sparks were already flying. He hoped his impulsiveness didn't get him burned but good this time.

After extracting a promise from Aaron that he would say nothing about her request of him, Shelby drove away from the station, where she'd come to get away from the resort for a little while. Whenever she needed a break from family and chores, she headed to town for a cherry freeze. She'd never expected to be followed home this time by Andrew Walker's identical twin brother.

Every time she thought of the way she'd thrown herself at him, she felt her face warm again. And not only from embarrassment. Remembering how his arms had gone obligingly around her, drawing her against that very fine, fit body, she felt a wave of heat climb from somewhere deep inside her all the way to her cheeks. Funny, she'd hugged Andrew when he'd left last year, standing in line with the rest of the family to do so, but she didn't remember having a reaction anything like this! Was it because there had been so many other people around? Because she had considered herself in a relationship with Pete then, tenuous as it had been? Or because there was some fundamental difference between Aaron and Andrew other than the way they wore their hair?

She couldn't wait to see how the rest of the family reacted to meeting him.

Turning off the two-lane highway onto the resort's entrance road, she drove the short distance to the gate booth. The family employed teenagers and senior citizens in part-time positions at the booth. Overnight guests of the resort were issued passes to allow them entrance, but day users of the boat launch, picnic or swimming areas were charged five dollars' admission per vehicle.

She spoke through her open car window to the seventysomething man currently working the booth. "The man in the car behind me is a guest, Mac. Wave him on through, okay?"

"Will do, Shelby."

The paved road forked just beyond the gate. Staying straight led to the campground—forty RV and camper sites with concrete pads and electric and water hookups, and a central unpaved area for more basic tent-camping enthusiasts. Half of the RV slots were waterfront sites, while the others were shaded by trees, within view and easy walking distance of the lake. Shelby turned right, driving past the boat-and-trailer parking lot toward the large L-shaped building that housed the offices, marina, a diner and a convenience store offering food and camping and fishing supplies. Behind the boat-trailer parking lot was a grassy compound holding a large pavilion, charcoal grills, tennis and basketball courts, and a children's playground. The pavilion was often rented out for family and high school reunions, corporate and church functions, and birthday parties. Even a few weddings had taken place there.

The marina lay straight ahead of her, with the boat dock, gas pump, lighted fishing pier and fish-cleaning station directly behind it. To the right of the marina was a large, sparkling swimming pool next to a two-story, sixteen-unit waterfront motel. Across the parking lot from the motel were three of the eight rustic cabins in the resort.

The road made a left turn in front of the marina, leading to the boat launch, a swimming area with a sandy beach, day-use grounds with picnic tables and a volleyball court, five waterfront cabins and the campgrounds. Public restrooms and shower facilities were strategically located in the resort for use by swimmers and campers who didn't have their own camper lavatories.

Following the circular road back around toward the gate, guests would pass a turn-off marked with a sign that read Private Drive. That narrow road led to three brick houses occupied by Shelby's parents, grandparents, and aunt and uncle. Her grandparents' house sat in the center, flanked on either side by the houses built by their sons. Shelby had lived in her parents' house from birth until she graduated from college four years ago, spending her entire life within the resort compound.

Near the three houses, a small, nicely landscaped compound held four tidy single-wide mobile homes. One of those mobile homes was Shelby's. The other three belonged to her brother, her cousin Maggie and her cousin Hannah.

Hannah's home was the newest. She'd had it moved in after her divorce sixteen months ago. She and her husband—"the evil ex," as he was known in the family—had both worked for the resort...well, Hannah had worked, and Wade pretended to be useful while secretly embezzling and scheming to get his hands on even more of the family's hard-earned profits. During their two-and-a-half-year marriage, Hannah and Wade lived in town and drove to the resort every day, but after the split, Hannah had needed the comfort of family around her. Not to mention that the divorce had cost her nearly everything she'd earned and saved, so moving back had been a financial benefit, too. Like the others, hers was a two-bedroom mobile home, which would come in handy soon.

Shelby didn't bother driving around to her place, but parked in front of the office, motioning for Aaron to pull in beside her.

"Let's get you set up for your stay," she said when they'd both emerged from their vehicles. "Would you rather have a motel room or a cabin? Because it's a weekday, we have several motel rooms available— probably one with a balcony looking out over the lake. Each room has a minifridge, flat-screen TV, cable and Wi-Fi, but no cooking facilities. I know one of the cabins across from the motel is unoccupied at the moment, but if you want a cabin, you'd probably rather have one on the water. I think there's a one-bed cabin there you could use. All the cabins have TV, cable, Wi-Fi and a full kitchenette. We provide linens and kitchenware, but guests supply their own food."

As she spoke Aaron studied the nearby pool in which several younger kids splashed noisily under the supervision of sunbathing parents, then turned in a circle to take in as much of the rest of the resort and lake as he could see from their vantage point. "That cabin on the water sounds good, if it's available," he said, proving he'd been listening while he looked. "I can go back into town for supplies after I unpack."

She motioned toward the large, multiwindowed main building with its double-glass-door entrance. "We sell a few groceries, just the basics for easy meals. We also have a small grill inside, open until 7:00 p.m. We serve burgers, sandwiches, hot dogs, salads and a soup of the day. Nothing fancy, but not bad. No need to drive back into town for food tonight unless you just want to."

He nodded. "That sounds great, thanks for the tip."

"Well, look who's here!" Bryan Bell ambled up to join them, a gas-powered weed trimmer dangling from a harness strapped around him. A lean fifty-three, with kind blue eyes and thinning sandy hair under a green cap emblazoned with the name and logo of the resort, Bryan was red-faced and sweaty from working in the heat. His sweat-dampened green T-shirt also bore the resort logo—the words *Bell Resort and Marina* printed inside a stylized, bell-shaped outline. The legs of his faded jeans were covered with grass clippings and dirt. Though everyone fussed at him for attempting too much during the worst heat of the day, her uncle was somewhat obsessive when it came to keeping the grounds trimmed and tidy.

Bryan beamed at Aaron. "Good to see you, Andrew. We've all been hoping you'd take us up on our offer to come stay with us. Did you bring fishing gear? If not, I'll fix you up. Take you out to my secret fishing hole in the morning."

For the first of what she was sure would be many times, Shelby said, "This isn't Andrew, Uncle Bryan. It's his twin brother, Aaron Walker. Aaron, meet my uncle, Bryan Bell."

Bryan blinked a couple of times, looking as startled

as Shelby herself had been. "Twin brother? Huh. Folks say Shelby's dad and I look alike, but we don't hold a candle to you and Andrew. Spitting image."

Aaron nodded patiently. "Identical twins."

"Well, ain't that something. So how is Andrew?"

"He's doing well, thank you for asking."

"Good to hear it. He going to be joining you?" Bryan asked hopefully.

Aaron shook his head. "I doubt it. He's pretty busy at work. I'm taking a couple weeks' vacation."

"Oh. Sorry to hear that." Apparently realizing what he'd just said, Bryan added hastily, "Not that we're sorry you're here. It's real good to meet you, Aaron. Andrew's family is as welcome here as he is. Nice of him to recommend us to you."

Aaron cleared his throat. "I was just going to check in."

"Don't let me keep you. And that fishing invitation is still good, by the way. I'll be down at the boat dock at around seven in the morning if you want to join me." Bryan grinned crookedly. "You've just got to sign in blood that you won't tell anyone about my hidey-hole— well, except maybe your brother. We owe him that much and more."

"I'll take you up on that," Aaron agreed congenially. "It's been too long since I've gone fishing."

"Who's that you're talking to, Bryan?" Dixie Bell, the seventy-nine-year-old matron of the family, had just come out of the office door. Silver-haired and brightly dressed, as always, she peered at Aaron through her rhinestone-enhanced glasses, then clapped her hands together, her lined face lighting up. "Well, as I live and breathe, it's Andrew. Aren't you a sight for sore eyes, young man. Come give Mimi a hug."

Claiming that her given name had always been a trial for her, especially combined with her married surname, Dixie had adopted the name Mimi with the birth of her first grandchild, Hannah, twenty-eight years ago. She insisted everyone she particularly liked should call her that. Andrew had been one of the chosen.

"It isn't Andrew, Mom."

Speaking at the same time as her uncle, Shelby said, "This is Aaron, Mimi. Andrew's twin brother."

Her grandmother frowned and looked over the tops of her glasses, studying Aaron's face intently. "Are you sure?"

Aaron made a sound that might have been a swallowed chuckle. "Yes, ma'am. I'm sure."

Mimi still didn't look entirely convinced. "Twin brother, you say? Andrew never mentioned he had a twin brother."

Shelby thought Aaron looked less than surprised by that omission. Didn't the brothers get along?

"I guess the subject never came up," he said.

"He told you all about us, hmm?"

"Really nice place you have here, Mrs. Bell. I'd like to stay a few days if you have a vacancy."

"Of course we have a vacancy for Andrew's brother," Mimi assured him, patting his arm. She didn't even seem to notice that he had made no attempt to respond to her question, though Shelby had taken note. "Cabin Eight has just been renovated, a job that didn't take as long as we expected, so we haven't booked it for the next week. We'll set you up in there. You stay as long as you want, no charge. It's a one-bedroom, but if that twin of yours wants to join you, there's a pullout sofa bed in the main room."

"It sounds ideal, but I will be paying for my stay

here," Aaron said firmly. "Your arrangement with Andrew is between you and him, but I've come for a vacation and I'll pay my way."

Mimi frowned at him in a battle of wills that few
people had the nerve to engage with her. Aaron held his
own, gazing back at her with a pleasant but utterly determined expression. After a moment, the older woman
harrumphed. "Shelby, take him inside and get him his
key. Have Lori take his credit card information, if he
insists, but give him the senior citizen discount."

Aaron chuckled. "I'll accept that."

Shelby felt a warm shiver slide through her in response to his laugh. She didn't remember hearing Andrew laugh quite that way. If he had, she certainly
hadn't responded as dramatically.

Having Aaron here was going to be interesting. And
not just because he had agreed to keep an eye on the
man in Cabin Seven.

She motioned for him to follow her into the office.
"Let's get that key."

Shelby rode with Aaron in his car to show him his
cabin, telling him she'd walk back to the office afterward. Cabin Eight was a pretty little A-frame nestled
at the edge of the lake, the last in a row of five cabins
of varying styles and sizes. Behind the cabins, a short
slope led straight down to the water, with a narrow,
graveled beach for walking or bank-fishing. A couple
of good-sized trees shaded the cabin's tiny side yard,
where a charcoal grill and concrete picnic table invited
casual cookouts. On the other side of a stand of trees
was the first of the line of waterside camper sites. An
enormous motor home with hydraulic extensions that

expanded the interior space was just visible through the ruffling leaves of the trees.

Really roughing it, Aaron thought with a chuckle, looking away from the luxury RV. He'd always preferred camping with a tent and a backpack himself—though he had to admit the little A-frame cabin was appealing. Quaint, his mom would call it. He suspected his mother would already have her camera out, snapping shots of the cabin and the picturesque lake spreading beyond, where wake-trailing boats and rooster-tail-spouting personal watercraft crisscrossed the deeply blue water.

A pretty brunette in a green golf cart parked at the end of the cabin's short driveway. "I see the dashing P.I. has returned," she called out with a grin. "It's good to see you again, Andrew—as long as no one's trying to bankrupt us again. Please tell me you're here for vacation, not business."

"This isn't Andrew, Maggie," Shelby corrected with a wry smile for Aaron. "It's his brother, Aaron."

Maggie laughed heartily. "Right. One of your practical jokes, Shelby? Trying to convince me he's undercover or something? A different name to go with the more casual clothes and longer hair—which I approve, by the way. Looks good."

Although he should be getting tired of identifying himself to these people, Aaron couldn't help but smile in response to Maggie's teasing tone. "Thanks. My brother is always after me to get a haircut."

Maggie frowned a little, as if something in his voice or behavior surprised her.

"It's not a joke, Maggie. This really is Andrew's brother, Aaron," Shelby insisted to her cousin. "He's going to stay with us for a few days."

Tilting her head, Maggie studied him intently. Aaron figured he might as well return the favor. Maggie didn't look much like Shelby, though there were some vague family resemblances. Her hair was straighter, darker—walnut-brown with golden streaks that could have come from the sun or a bottle, for all he knew. Unlike Shelby's bright blue eyes, Maggie's were hazel, framed in thick, dark lashes. Definitely attractive, but he still found himself more intrigued by Shelby.

"You're Andrew's brother," Maggie said.

Shelby shook her head with an exasperated sigh. "That's what I just told you. Geez, Mags."

"Well, how was I to know you weren't kidding? I mean, they look exactly alike. Mostly."

Exactly, mostly. Aaron had to laugh at that. "It's nice to meet you, Maggie."

"Back at you, Aaron. Is Andrew here, too?"

"No, he's working in Dallas."

"Oh. Well, tell him I said hello, will you?"

"I'll do that."

With a wave, she started the golf cart again and headed down the road into the camping area.

"So, can I expect a variation of that conversation with all the rest of your relatives?" he asked Shelby.

She pushed a hand through her blond curls and gave him an apologetic smile. "I'll try to spread the word before you run into the rest of them. They will, however, treat you like an old friend, just because you're Andrew's brother."

He was unable to completely suppress a wince. "Yes, well, I'll be sure and tell him everyone says hello."

And he would not tell the Bell family he'd learned about their resort from a brochure he'd found lying next to Andrew's trash can.

Shelby studied him a bit too closely for comfort before stepping onto the tiny front porch to unlock the door of the cabin. "Andrew stayed in the motel when he was here last summer. He said he didn't need a kitchen because he didn't cook, that all he needed was a bed and a table for his computer. But then, he was working, not vacationing."

Aaron tried to remember when his brother had last taken a vacation. Had it been their hiking trip with their cousin Casey in Tennessee just over a year ago? That would have been before whatever job Andrew had done for the Bell family. It seemed like especially the past six months or so—since around Christmas, perhaps— Andrew had done nothing but work like a demon. And criticize his brother for not doing the same, of course. Even though Aaron had worked damned hard for the commercial real estate firm where he'd spent the past year, and had been successful enough in it that he could get by for a few months before running through his savings, his heart just hadn't been in that career, something Andrew had predicted from the start.

"I like to cook sometimes. Nothing fancy, but it usually turns out pretty good." He looked around the interior of the cabin in approval.

Though small, the space was well designed. The open living space was separated from the kitchen by an eating bar with two tall stools. A door to his left probably led into a bathroom, and a flight of wooden steps led up to the sleeping loft. A sofa, an armchair and a wooden rocker provided plenty of seating, and a flat-screen TV hung on the wall. The furniture looked new, as did the gleaming wood floor. A sliding glass door at the back of the room provided a view of a back deck and the lake. Two teenagers on Jet Skis sped past as he looked that way, but the cabin was insulated well enough to mute outside sounds.

"This is nice."

Shelby smiled. "It's the smallest of the cabins, but one of my favorites. We get a lot of honeymooners in this one. You lucked out that it's available now. It took some water damage in that big spring wind storm last month, and we didn't expect it to be available again until the first of July."

He glanced around again, seeing no evidence of damage. "I remember the reports of that storm. Cut a swath across this part of the state, didn't it? Was there much damage to the resort?"

"Luckily, no. A lot of stuff was tossed around, but this cabin took the only real damage when a large tree limb fell on the roof. It looked really bad at first, but most of the damage was cosmetic. Fortunately, the cabin was unoccupied at the time, and we've had a tree service out since to take down any other branches that pose a hazard." She laughed and shook her head. "Uncle Bryan wanted to climb the trees and take the limbs down himself, but the rest of the family overruled him on that. He's very territorial about the grounds."

"I assume everyone in the family has a specific job here?" It was that way at D'Alessandro-Walker. Various family members worked in management, investigations, customer service, administrative and IT jobs. He'd tried most of them himself.

Shelby nodded. "Uncle Bryan and my brother, Steven, are in charge of the grounds and general maintenance. My dad mans the marina. Mom and Aunt Linda run the store and the grill. Maggie hires and supervises the housekeeping staff, and Hannah works in the office, taking reservations and handling promotion. My sister,

Lori, helps out when she's home from college, and my grandparents stay busy wherever they're needed. They never let us forget they were the ones who started this enterprise," she added with a crooked smile.

"You didn't mention what your job is," he reminded her.

"I keep the books. I'm a CPA."

That surprised him. "You look too young to have earned a CPA."

"I'm almost twenty-six. We were all expected to attend college," she explained. "Most of us majored in business courses, though Lori keeps changing her major. I think she's had three so far. None of which would be particularly useful for working in the family business. Which, I suppose, is her point."

Aaron thought it possible he shared a bit in common with Lori, though he chose to keep that observation to himself. "Will Lori work for the resort when she graduates?"

"I don't know. She won't commit yet, though she's always willing to fill in during holidays and summer breaks. She's running the office while Maggie's away for a few weeks. Steven—" Shelby gave a little sigh. "I think Steven might have liked to try something else, had he not felt so much pressure to help out around here. Just about the time he earned his business degree, the local economy took a hit and it became even more important for us to keep a tight rein on the resort expenses, salaries, benefits, that sort of thing. That was why it hit us so hard that the evil ex was willing to clean us out if he could've gotten away with it."

Even more reason for the family's gratitude toward Andrew, Aaron mused. "So, did you ever think about leaving the family business yourself?" he asked casually.

She adjusted a lamp into a more secure position on a rustic end table. "Not really. I've always known this is where I belong. My family's a little different, but then so I am. We're close and we get along very well, for the most part. I like my work, and the people we meet here in the resort. Well, most of the people," she added darkly, glancing toward the tiny round kitchen window, through which Cabin Seven was just visible.

Following her gaze, he asked, "Is that where the 'hinky' guy is staying?"

"Yes. Which makes it all the more convenient that you're in this one."

He wasn't sure *convenient* was the word he'd have used. He didn't relish the image of himself sneaking peeks at his neighbor during his impulsive vacation. He moved to look out the window, just to ascertain how much he could see from here. Shelby followed him, standing shoulder to shoulder with him as they gazed out at the slightly larger cabin next door. The blinds were all closed, so they were unable to see in, though he wasn't sure how much he could have made out, anyway, through the lightly tinted glass. He spotted movement from the corner of his eye and automatically turned his head to look that direction.

A tall, thin man with buzz-cut hair, a square jaw and a stern expression half hidden by oversized mirrored aviator glasses stood at the back of Cabin Seven, as if he'd just walked up from the lakeshore. Obviously he'd noticed them looking at his cabin, because he'd stopped to glare at them. Aaron gave him a friendly nod, then drew Shelby away from the window.

"You haven't actually expressed your concerns to

Landon, have you?" he asked her, thinking of the other man's suspicious scowl.

"No, of course not! Though, maybe…"

He raised his eyebrows. "Maybe…?" he prodded.

Looking a bit sheepish, she scuffed the toe of one flip-flop against the floor. "Well, maybe he's noticed me looking at him a few times. I mean, I think I've been discreet about it."

Aaron had a strong suspicion that *discreet* and *Shelby* were two words rarely used in the same sentence. He shook his head. "I'll unpack, then head over to the grill for something to eat before they close. If I happen to notice anything nefarious going on in the cabin next door, I'll be sure and let you know."

She gave him a quick frown, as if trying to determine if she was being mocked, but then she laughed. "Okay, you do that," she said good-naturedly. "Maybe we should have a secret code word."

"Nebraska," he suggested, because for some reason that was the first word that popped into his mind.

Giggling, she nodded and moved toward the door. "Right. If I hear you say *Nebraska,* I'll know you found signs of nefariousness. Um, *nefariousness* is a word, right?"

He shrugged. "Sure, why not?"

"And we need another code word for danger," she suggested, carrying the teasing a bit further. "Since we're naming states, how about Minnesota?"

"*Minnesota* sounds very ominous," he agreed, tongue-in-cheek. "If I ever feel in danger, I'll say *Minnesota.*"

"And I'll rush to your rescue." She paused with a hand on the doorknob, looking over her shoulder at him with a bright smile. "So, I'll see you later?"

"You will most definitely see me later," he assured her.

He was gratified by the slight wave of pink in her cheeks when she slipped out the door. Maybe there had been no sparks between Shelby and Andrew—but he didn't think he was imagining the sizzle between her and himself. And while it was unlikely that the attraction would lead to anything, considering that they were surrounded by her entire family, he certainly wouldn't mind flirting with her while he was here, however long that might be.

He drew his phone out of his pocket. He needed to let the family know he was out of town for a few days. And he had a few questions for his twin.

Chapter Three

"Where the hell are you?" Andrew demanded in lieu of a greeting when he answered his phone.

"I'm fine, bro, thanks for asking."

Andrew didn't bother to respond to Aaron's sarcastic comment. "Everyone was expecting you at the graduation party for Miles last night. Mom said you called her and told her you were headed out of town for a few days, but she thought you'd wait until after the party to leave. Dad's ticked at you for just taking off without telling anyone where you were going."

"I told them I wasn't in the mood for a party. I specifically said I wouldn't be there."

"They thought you'd change your mind. Mom seemed really surprised when you didn't show up."

"I'm sure there were plenty of people there to celebrate the occasion," Aaron muttered, pushing down a ripple of defensive guilt. "I sent Miles a graduation gift."

There was always some sort of family gathering in the extended Walker clan. A birthday, an anniversary, a wedding, a housewarming, a birth. He and Andrew had thirteen first cousins just on their dad's side, and another generation was well underway. The family had gathered last night at their cousin Brynn Walker D'Alessandro's house to commemorate the high school graduation of Brynn and Joe's son, Miles. So not only would many of the Walkers have been in attendance, but a good number of D'Alessandros had also been invited.

Even knowing he risked general disapproval with his absence, Aaron just couldn't make himself attend. It had been about the time he should have been leaving for the party when he'd impulsively decided to escape to the lake for a few days. Someplace where no one would know him or any other member of his illustrious family. He guessed the joke was on him.

"So, Andrew. Tell me about the Bell family."

A rather lengthy silence followed before Andrew cleared his throat and asked, "The Bell family?"

"Bell Resort and Marina? I'd think you'd remember, since you are apparently the Bell family hero."

"Tell me you aren't at the resort."

"I could tell you that, but it would be a lie. I needed a place to get away for a few days. I'm sure you can figure out why. I didn't expect to be greeted with genuflects when the folks here mistook me for you."

"How did you end up there, anyway?"

"I found a brochure in—well, near your trash can yesterday. It looked ideal, and since you'd thrown the brochure away, I figured you weren't interested and I wouldn't have to worry about running into you or the rest of the family. I'd be completely anonymous. As usual, my plan didn't work out quite as I expected."

"Well, what do you expect?" Andrew asked with unmistakable exasperation. "You take off out of the blue to someplace you learn about from my trash can and you're surprised there are complications?"

"I just needed to get away to think." Aaron hated that he'd gone on the defensive, as he so often did with his twin lately. "It's no different from what Casey did when he was questioning his career with the law firm in Dallas. He spent some meditation time in east Tennessee away from the family pressure for a few weeks and it ended up working out great for him. He met Natalie, they went into legal practice together, they've been happily married for—what? Four years now?"

"So you headed for southeast Texas looking for a wife?"

Aaron scowled. He was rapidly growing tired of his brother's sarcasm. "I just need to reassess. Granted, I didn't know there would be all new expectations of me here, just because I happen to be your brother."

"What expectations?"

"We'll get to that in a minute. First, why don't you tell me exactly what you did for the Bell family that made them all so grateful to you? Were you just doing the job, or did you go beyond the call of duty to reap all this gratitude?"

"They hired me to assist with a problem and I took care of it. It wasn't a favor—they paid me for my time, though they gave me so many perks at the resort that I took a discount off the total bill. And you know I'm not going to discuss the details of the case with you, Aaron."

Aaron was not surprised by Andrew's insistence on client confidentiality, even under these circumstances. "Shelby told me the basics of your job for them last summer, so you wouldn't be breaking any agency rules to talk about it superficially with me. But I'm not really all that interested in your case. Tell me about Shelby."

"Shelby?" Andrew's brusque voice softened. "She's sort of flaky, but a sweetheart, really. She gets a little carried away. Takes an idea and runs with it. She really got into the investigation when I was there. Came up with a lot of increasingly improbable ideas for helping me, that sort of thing."

Something about his brother's indulgent tone rubbed Aaron the wrong way. He found himself getting defensive on Shelby's behalf. "Are you saying she can't be taken seriously?"

"No, I didn't say that. Shelby's damn good at her accounting job for the resort. She's the one who figured out what was going on with the guy they all call 'the evil ex,' even though she couldn't find the proof they needed without professional help. And a couple of her offbeat ideas came in rather helpful when we were laying a trap for the jerk. She just goes about things a little differently. So what's going on with her?"

"She asked me to look into one of the guests here. She thought I was you at the time she asked, but even after I corrected her, she thought I'd be qualified to do some snooping."

Andrew groaned. "What sort of snooping?"

Aaron filled him in on Shelby's concerns and her reasoning behind them. He could almost hear Andrew shaking his head before he finished. "Don't let her drag you into one of her convoluted plots, Aaron. There are things here you need to do—like find a new job. Dad's already got some prospects lined up for you."

Aaron wondered if maybe he'd be more successful in any future career efforts if he lined up his own prospects. "I'll call Dad later," he said, somewhat curtly. "In the meantime, how about you run a name for me?"

"The hinky guy?"

"Yeah. No harm in checking him out, is there?"

"Give me his name," Andrew said in resignation.

"Terrence Landon. And I've got a license plate. There's a black SUV parked in front of his cabin."

A heavy sigh sounded in his ear after he'd rattled off the numbers. "I'll see what I can find. For Shelby," Andrew added.

"I'm sure she'd appreciate it. Hell, she and the family will probably rename the resort in your honor."

"Very funny. Um—have you met all the family yet?"

"Not all. A few. Had to convince the ones I've met that I'm not really you in disguise."

"Have you met Hannah?"

Hannah. Running through a quick mental rundown of Shelby's chatter about her family, Aaron remembered that Hannah was Shelby's cousin, Maggie's sister. "No. Shelby said Hannah is out of the state for a couple of weeks, visiting her mother's relatives. A vacation from the vacation spot, I guess."

"I see." Andrew didn't sound amused. "I'll check this name and get back to you. You call Dad and explain why you've decided now is a good time to take off on a fishing trip."

"And maybe you should consider seeing someone about having that stick up your backside removed," Aaron snapped back. "Seems like it's been getting more firmly lodged lately."

He shoved his phone into his pocket before his brother could reply to the rather juvenile taunt. His temper sizzled. Andrew had a lot of nerve acting like Mr. Responsibility these days. Despite his rather recently adopted sanctimonious tone, Andrew had caused more than a few parental headaches of his own, despite excelling from a young age at D'Alessandro-Walker. Most likely because he'd known from the time he was a kid that he wanted to be an investigator.

Aaron didn't know for certain what he wanted to do next, but he was sure of one thing—it wouldn't be in the family business where so many people felt they had the right to tell him what to do.

Glancing at the bags still sitting on the floor, he stepped around them. He would unpack later. Maybe. He was beginning to wonder if he should just move on to someplace where he wouldn't be walking in Andrew's footsteps.

"He really looks that much like Andrew?"

Both Shelby and her grandmother nodded in response to the question from Shelby's mother. Leaning her elbows on the polished counter of the Chimes Grill, Shelby said, "It will blow your mind."

The Chimes Grill was located in one end of the big two-story main building. Decorated in a retro, red-and-chrome '50s theme, it held eight red-laminate-topped chrome tables with red vinyl seating and framed '50s movie posters on the crisp white walls. A little clichéd, maybe, but they liked it, and so did their guests. The long bar where Shelby sat was also red-topped, with six swivel stools. Her mother bustled around the open cooking area that filled the little diner with tempting aromas, skillfully flipping cooked patties onto waiting buns, which she would top with onion, lettuce and tomato. Pickle spears and chips were served on the side. A warming pot held the soup du jour, vegetable beef today. Homemade pies and soft-freeze ice cream were popular desserts.

The menu was simple and limited, but they didn't lack for customers from among the campers, guests and day-use visitors. Two couples and one family of four were enjoying early dinners, and two fishermen swapped ones-that-got-away lies over coffee at the other end of the bar.

"I knew almost immediately he wasn't Andrew," Mimi said, absently polishing her sparkly glasses on her red-and-purple-flowered blouse. "I mean, at first glance there are similarities, but once I got a good look at him, I knew."

Shelby rolled her eyes while her mom and her aunt Linda shared knowing smiles they had the sense to hide from their mother-in-law. "Mimi, you demanded that he give you a hug."

"That was before I saw him full-on," her grandmother answered serenely.

"You asked him if he was sure he wasn't Andrew."

Shelby's mother chuckled, though she swallowed the laugh almost immediately when Mimi gave her a stern look.

"He does look very much like Andrew, but there are quite a few differences." Mimi slipped her glasses onto her nose and nodded firmly at her daughters-in-law. "You'll see."

There were differences, Shelby thought. The longer hair, the more casual clothing—but she sensed that the real dissimilarity between Aaron and Andrew went deeper than physical. She was eager to study those differences more closely. Just for curiosity, of course.

Leaving Shelby sitting at the end of the counter, her mom moved away to take an order from a sunburned couple who'd spent the day on the water and were now hungry for burgers. Seeing some customers entering, Linda headed back into the store, and Mimi went to the office to check on Lori, who was answering phones today. Home for the summer before her junior year of college, Lori was filling in for Hannah. Having grown up working around the resort, Lori didn't really need supervision in the office, but their grandmother watched over every aspect of the business as if she was the only one who could truly be in charge. "Pop," as her husband, the patriarch, was known, tended to bark orders and strut around the grounds, but everyone knew Mimi was the one with the real power in the family.

Though it was already after five, Shelby had just a few things to do yet, but she wasn't quite ready to settle in front of the computer. She wasn't a rigid eight-to-five type, working whatever hours she needed to put in to get her job done efficiently, and the family didn't have a problem with her unconventional schedule. They knew she would put in as much time as needed. Like everyone else in the family, she tended to work a good ten or fifteen hours a week over the standard forty. And she loved it.

Twisting on the red-vinyl-topped bar stool, she cast a proprietary gaze around her. Through the open doors of the grill, she could see the entry foyer into the main building. The foyer was decorated with mounted fish, antique lures displayed on wooden plaques and lush, live greenery. At the back of the foyer, facing the main doors, was the reception office where Lori was working. The other offices, including Shelby's, were upstairs, accessible to family only. Opposite the grill, the convenience store was lined with shelves of groceries, souvenirs, camping and fishing supplies. The store opened at the back into the marina, where Shelby's dad, with rotating help from his brother and son, sold bait, fuel, motor oil and other marine supplies; rented out fishing boats, ski boats, pontoon boats and personal watercraft; and kept an eye on the boat slips and fishing pier.

The resort had been Shelby's playground as a child—the campgrounds and pier, the pool and tennis courts, even the store and the grill. She'd scooped minnows for customers by the time she was eight, served ice cream when she was ten, cleaned motel rooms when she hit her teens. Her siblings and cousins could make the same claims, and Steven could have added that he had twice saved children from drowning in the lake.

She remembered Aaron asking if she'd ever thought of leaving the business. She'd been completely honest when she'd told him that she had not. Unlike her brother and sister, she thought with a faint sigh. The whole family had begun to sense Steven's restlessness, and Lori refused to commit her future to the resort until she'd explored a few other options.

"What are you thinking about so hard?" her mother asked, wandering back to where Shelby sat. "You're not still fretting about the man in Cabin Seven, are you?" she added in a whisper, glancing around to make sure none of her customers overheard the question.

"Not at the moment."

Her mother narrowed her eyes suspiciously. Dark blond hair pulled back into a casual twist, blue-eyed, fresh-faced, fifty-two-year-old Sarah Clements Bell had been mistaken more than once for an older sibling to her three grown offspring. She dressed neatly but casually in resort-logo polo shirts and khakis, wore a minimum of makeup, eschewed jewelry except for her watch, wedding rings and simple stud earrings, and refused to fret about maintaining the perfect figure, though she was probably less than twenty pounds over the ideal weight for her average height. Her husband thought she was the most beautiful woman in the world, and her children adored her, but none of them made the mistake of underestimating her.

"Shelby, what have you done?" she asked in a low, firm voice. "You haven't hired an investigator to check out your suspicions, have you? Is that why Aaron Walker came here?"

"No, Mom, that's not why he came," Shelby replied, able to look her mother straight in the eyes because that was, of course, the truth. She saw no need to mention the invitation she'd mailed to Andrew recently. How could she have known his brother would show up instead?

She should have realized she wouldn't get away with the prevarication. "Did you tell him your theories when you took him down to his cabin?" her mom persisted. "Please tell me you didn't ask him to spy on the neighboring cabin."

Shelby cleared her throat.

"Shelby!" her mother hissed in exasperation, darting another quick look around. "We can't talk about this now, but you can bet we will be discussing it as soon as we're in private."

"All I did was ask him to keep an eye out while he's here," Shelby muttered, feeling entirely too much like a kid in trouble. "It's not like I officially hired him or anything. He said he didn't mind."

"You imposed on his vacation by—oh, my goodness."

Her mother was looking beyond her, toward the doorway, and Shelby had a sudden inkling of what had caused the startled expression. She swiveled on her seat, then nodded at Aaron as he slid onto the stool next to her. "Didn't take you long to unpack."

"That's because I haven't yet," he replied with a shrug. "I was talking to my brother."

And it hadn't been a warm and fuzzy call, Shelby mused, studying Aaron's expression. Something was definitely going on between the brothers, and she didn't think it took a P.I. to figure that out.

"Mom, this is Aaron Walker. Aaron, my mother, Sarah Bell."

"It's very nice to meet you," her mother said, shaking his hand. "Welcome to the resort."

"Thank you, Mrs. Bell."

"Please, call me Sarah. Can I get you anything?"

He glanced at the menu over the grill. "A grilled chicken sandwich sounds good."

"Shelby, why don't you serve Aaron something to drink while I cook his sandwich?"

He requested a lemonade, which Shelby fetched swiftly from a pitcher behind the counter. "I've been trying to prepare everyone for seeing you," she informed him as she set the plastic tumbler in front of him. "You'll probably still get a few double takes."

He shrugged. "I'm used to that."

She studied his handsome face from beneath her lashes. "I'll just bet you are," she murmured.

His eyebrows rose, and he studied her speculatively.

Giving him a friendly pat on the shoulder, she said, "Enjoy your dinner. Mom will take good care of you. I have some things to wrap up in my office, but I'll see you later."

She heard his stool squeak when he turned to watch

her stroll toward the exit. She added a little extra pop to her walk—just because.

She hadn't flirted this way with Andrew, she remembered, her amusement fading. Because of Pete, maybe. Or maybe the circumstances. But she couldn't resist drawing those lazy grins from Aaron that made him look so different from his brother. And now she sounded like Mimi, she thought with a wry shake of her head.

It wasn't as if she expected anything to happen between her and Aaron. He was here for vacation, and he'd agreed to do a favor for her only because she'd given him little choice. She wasn't the type to sweep a good-looking adventurer, which she considered Aaron to be, off his feet. She wasn't the "pretty one" in the family—her cousin Hannah held that title. Nor was she the summer-fling type. She'd had plenty of opportunities for that sort of thing, had she been interested, but that just wasn't her style. Still, she enjoyed a little harmless flirtation as much as the next girl, especially with a man as attractive as Aaron Walker. Those sexy smiles of his were definitely rewards in themselves.

Half an hour later, after finishing the few work tasks she'd had left to do that day, she wandered back downstairs—only to find Aaron still in the diner, now sitting at a table surrounded by members of her family. Maggie sat next to him, with Mimi on his other side. All three of them were eating her mom's homemade chocolate pie. Uncle Bryan and Aunt Linda sat across the table with cups of coffee. With no one waiting to order at the moment, Sarah sat on a bar stool near the table, participating in the lively conversation.

Shelby noted that Aaron didn't seem to be saying much—as if anyone could get a word in edgewise with her family—but he appeared to be enjoying himself.

She moved toward the cheery group. "Looks like a party going on in here."

Her aunt motioned her over. "We were just telling Aaron some funny stories about raising you kids in the resort. He said he and Andrew always had family around when they were growing up, too."

Aaron chuckled. "We could never get away with much. Which doesn't mean we didn't try. The terrible trio got into more than a few scrapes, despite being watched almost constantly by our parents, aunts and uncles. Not to mention older cousins who thought it was their job to report on our activities."

"The terrible trio?" Shelby asked, pulling up a chair.

He nodded. "That's what they called my brother, our cousin Casey and me. I can't imagine why," he added with a humorous attempt at innocence.

Mimi tsked her tongue. "I bet you boys were a handful."

"Yes, ma'am, we surely were."

Maggie propped her chin on her hand and studied Aaron with a smile. "For some reason, I can picture you getting up to mischief, but it surprises me that your brother was part of it. He seemed so proper and conservative."

"I guess he is. Now," Aaron murmured, and once again Shelby would have liked to know what was going on between the twins.

"Oh, here's Pop," Shelby's mom commented, glancing toward the doorway. "I don't think you've met my father-in-law, Aaron."

"No, I haven't." Aaron started to rise, but the older man waved him back into his seat, peering intently at Aaron's face.

Shelby sat back to enjoy the show.

Pop scraped a chair on the floor and dropped into it, never taking his gaze off Aaron. A sun-weathered, work-hardened eighty, Carl Bell Sr. had a ring of thin gray hair around his brown-spotted scalp and silver-framed glasses through which he peered with intense gray eyes. His nose was crooked and his thin mouth firm. He had hunched a bit with age, softened around the middle, and moved a bit more slowly, but he was still in full possession of his faculties. The thing was, Pop had always been eccentric, a quirk that grew more pronounced each year.

"So you're Aaron." He didn't quite make air quotes with his fingers, but the gesture seemed to be implied.

Aaron nodded. "Yes, sir."

"Humph." Pop narrowed his eyes, while everyone else watched with poorly suppressed smiles. "I imagine a P.I. might need to use a different name when he goes on vacation. What they call *incognito*."

"If he was incognito, why would he come to a place where everyone would recognize him, Pop?" Bryan asked.

Pop had never been overly concerned with logic. "Probably because he'd know he'd be among friends who wouldn't give him away if anyone asked. You got a picture of yourself with Andrew?" he asked their guest.

Aaron seemed amused. "No, sir, not with me."

"Humph," Pop said again and gave the others a somewhat smug glance.

Laughing, Linda stood. "I've got to go take care of a customer in the store. I'll let the rest of you try to convince Pop that identical twins do occur in nature."

"Pop tends to let his imagination get away with him. And most of us think Shelby is just like her grandfather," Shelby's mom confided to Aaron with a smile that was both affectionate and wry. Maybe it even held a bit of a warning, Shelby thought with a frown.

Was her mother actually cautioning Aaron that he couldn't take everything Shelby said seriously? *Well, gee, thanks for the support, Mom,* she tried to say with her expression.

If she received the subliminal message, Sarah ignored it serenely, moving to wait on an elderly couple who'd just come in for dinner. She greeted them by name. For almost as far back as Shelby could remember, the Hendersons had traveled in their motor home from Shreveport, Louisiana, at least a couple times a year for weeklong stays at the resort.

Lori drifted in through the diner doors, pausing to look with surprise at the group of relatives gathered there. "What's everyone doing in here? Oh." She pushed a fringe of blue-streaked black hair out of her eyes and studied the man everyone had gathered around. "You must be Andrew's brother. Mimi told me about you."

"Says he's an identical twin," Pop said with a grin and a broad wink, causing everyone to shake their heads in exasperation. "We've been instructed to call him Aaron."

Lifting a thin, arched brow, Lori glanced at Shelby, who shrugged. "Lori, this really is Aaron Walker. Aaron, my sister, Lori."

They exchanged greetings, and Shelby wondered idly what Aaron thought of Lori, who looked so different from the rest of the family—a deliberate effort on her part. Taller and thinner than Shelby, twenty-year-old Lori wore her colorful hair short and shaggy, tumbling into blue eyes lined in dark, smoky gray. She sported bloodred lipstick and black nail polish, and favored filmy, smoke-colored garments that seemed to float around her when she walked. She refused to call her style "Goth," saying the term was outdated and inaccurate. She liked to call her taste "ethereal" instead.

However it was defined, the style somehow worked for Lori. Shelby thought her sister looked striking and interesting, especially in comparison to her own wardrobe, which consisted primarily of easy-care shorts and T-shirts chosen for ease of movement and comfort in hot Texas summers. In the winters, she swapped the shorts for jeans, wore long-sleeved tees and donned sneakers rather than flip-flops. Glancing from Lori's ethereal chic, to Maggie's pretty, fitted wrap top and cropped khakis, Shelby wondered if maybe she should start paying a bit more attention to her own wardrobe.

Aaron pushed his chair back from the table. "It's been great meeting everyone, but I should probably unpack and make a few phone calls."

"Did you walk over?" Shelby asked.

When he nodded she stood. "I left my car here earlier. I can drop you off at your cabin on my way to my place."

She was aware that everyone watched them as they walked out. Did they think she was chasing after Aaron? She frowned, her ego piqued at the thought. She was going to have to think of a plan that would let her collaborate with Aaron while still preserving her feminine pride.

"So I've met everyone in the family except your father and brother now?" Aaron asked when they were in her car.

"And Hannah."

"But she's out of town."

"Right." Shelby started the engine. "Dad and Steven have been busy today. I'm sure you'll meet them tomorrow."

He nodded. "Have to admit I'll be glad when your whole family has seen me and gotten past the fact that I look like my brother."

She glanced at him apologetically as she backed out of the parking space. "I'm sorry about that. I'm sure you're getting tired of hearing it."

"Like I said, I'm used to it."

She thought of her sister's little rebellions against being surrounded by a sometimes-too-close family. How much more restless would Lori feel if she looked so much like her sister that no one could even tell them apart?

"So, about your grandfather."

"Pop?"

"Yeah. Is he serious? About insisting I'm really Andrew, I mean."

"Sometimes it's hard to tell with Pop," she admitted. "He can carry on a joke for days without ever cracking a smile. But he can also get an idea in his head that you couldn't shake with a jackhammer. If he's really decided you're Andrew, it would take the two of you standing side by side in front of him to convince him otherwise. And I'm not certain even that would do it," she added with a rueful laugh.

Aaron laughed with her. "He reminds me a little of Vinnie D'Alessandro. He's the grandfather of some of my cousins. Older than your Pop—Vinnie's over ninety—but just as pigheaded."

She stared fiercely out the windshield as she made the short drive to his cabin. "That, uh, crack my mom made. About me being like Pop?"

"I could tell that ticked you off."

Had she been so transparent? She hadn't even realized he was looking at her. "Anyway, I'm not imagining that there's something strange about Terrence Landon. Maybe he's not doing anything illegal, but he's definitely weird."

"You should probably not hang around staring at him unless you want him to disappear in the middle of the night or something. If he's up to something illegal, he'll bolt for fear that you're onto him. If he's not, he'll take off because you've creeped him out. Now, maybe it's your objective to get him to leave...."

She parked behind his car in the short driveway to his cabin. "No. I mean, if he's not up to anything...well, nefarious, as you called it, then I don't want to run off a paying customer."

"So you'll stop watching him and let me keep an eye out—maybe a bit more discreetly?"

"Actually, I've been thinking about that."

She heard a faint sound that might have been a muffled groan, and she shot a quick, suspicious look at Aaron, but his expression was bland. "What have you been thinking?" he asked a little warily.

"Well, I can see where it would look odd if I keep hanging around your place for no apparent reason. Landon could think I'm watching him, and other people—well, they might wonder if I'm chasing after you or something. Which I'm totally not doing," she assured him firmly.

Aaron nodded. His expression was still innocuous, but she thought she saw a new glint of amusement in his dark eyes, which only made her frown. "Anyway," she continued doggedly, "maybe if *you* could flirt with *me* a little—you know, like you're interested in me—I could act like I might be interested in return."

"A summer flirtation."

"Something like that," she agreed. "It would probably be more believable if you were hitting on Maggie, or even Lori, but neither of them are interested in finding out what's going on with Landon. Maggie thinks I'm letting my imagination run away with me and Lori just doesn't care, so neither of them would go along with it. Not that I'd want them to, anyway. I'm the one who noticed something off with the guy, and I want to find out for myself if my instincts were right again."

He followed her somewhat disjointed plan easily enough, apparently, though one comment seemed to particularly intrigue him. "Why would it be more believable if I was interested in your cousin or your sister? And by the way, I don't hit on young college students, regardless."

Nice to know, she thought. "Guys tend to notice Maggie. Well, when Hannah's not around, anyway. Hannah's the one who makes men walk into walls."

"And what about you?" he asked, studying her face a little too closely.

Shelby shrugged. "I'm everyone's pal. But just for the next few days, maybe you could pretend to flirt with me? That would give me a reason to hang around here some—if you don't mind, that is?"

"I wouldn't mind at all having you hang around me. And I don't think it would be such a hardship to flirt with you."

She giggled in response to his tone. "Thanks. I could probably use the practice. It's been a while since…"

She shook her head. "Anyway, we could kill several birds with one stone this way. We can keep an eye on Landon and if I'm right that he's using our resort for his own shady purposes, my family will have to admit that my instincts about people are better than they think. And I have to confess that having a good-looking guy like you flirting with me would be good for my ego. The family's been worried that my last boyfriend broke my heart when he dum—er, when we broke up a few months ago."

"Did he break your heart?"

Shelby sighed gustily. "No, he did not. Maybe he bruised my pride a little—I mean, I sort of selfishly wish I'd been the one to break it off first, but it was bound to happen eventually, anyway. Pete felt stifled by having my family around all the time, and he was impatient with my responsibilities to the resort, which keep me pretty busy. But if I spend a little time with you, and then politely break it off with you, they'll see that I'm in no hurry to get hooked up with anyone else. That I'm perfectly content with my life the way it is for now. That makes sense, right?"

"So, you're going to shoot me down in front of your family in order to convince them that you aren't looking for a man in your life."

She winced, but he seemed more amused than annoyed. "Well, yes. I guess that's a lot to ask."

"I'm starting to get used to it." Sitting sideways in the passenger seat, one arm draped behind him as he watched her, Aaron cocked his head. "Is everything an elaborate scheme with you?"

She shifted uncomfortably in her seat. "Not everything."

Looking away from his too-perceptive gaze, she saw the blinds twitch in the front window of Cabin Seven. "I think Landon is spying on us!" she said indignantly.

Aaron's laugh held an edge of recklessness. "Then maybe we should give him something worth seeing."

Before Shelby could question the comment, she found herself in Aaron's arms, her mouth smothered by his.

His lips were firm, warm, and there was just a hint of roughness to his chin, as if it had been several hours since he'd shaved. He smelled good, male and spicy. Her hands rested on his chest, but she had to make an effort not to wrap her arms around his neck and yank him across the console of the car.

Considering the explosions it ignited inside her, the kiss didn't actually last all that long. Aaron drew back with a smile. "That should give him something to think about."

It would certainly give her something to think about—perhaps even to dream about, she thought with a gulp. "Um—yeah."

"Good night, Shelby. I'll see you tomorrow."

"Good night, Aaron," she replied, somewhat surprised that her wildly tingling lips would even form coherent words.

He climbed out of the car and strolled to his front door with neither a glance toward the neighboring cabin nor back toward her. After a moment, Shelby roused herself to start her car and back carefully out of the drive.

Chapter Four

Aaron stepped out of his cabin at just before seven the next morning, filling his lungs with the crisp breeze coming off the lake. Though a few thin clouds drifted across the pale morning sky, it was going to be another beautiful day. It was already warm, but comfortably so this early. From the water came the growl of boat motors as fishermen headed out for their anticipated catch.

Carrying his fishing rod in one hand and tackle box in the other, he headed for the marina. He wore jeans and a gray pocket T-shirt with battered sneakers. A Texas Rangers ball cap shielded his face from the rising sun, though he hadn't yet donned the sunglasses tucked into his shirt pocket.

The marina smelled of fuel, exhaust and vaguely of fish, a combination that took him back to fishing outings of the past. He didn't see Shelby's uncle Bryan, but a man who bore a strong familial resemblance was sweeping the pier with a push broom. The man looked around when Aaron approached, giving him a thorough once-over.

"You must be Andrew's brother," he drawled. "Heard about you."

"And you must be Bryan's brother," Aaron responded with a faint smile. "I heard about you, too."

"Carl Jr. But you can call me C.J. Been nicknamed that since I was a kid."

Aaron nodded. "Nice to meet you, C.J."

"Everyone says you're as likable as your brother— well, everyone except Pop, who seems to think you *are* your brother."

"So I gathered." Chuckling, Aaron set down his tackle box. "Bryan invited me to fish with him this morning. Have you seen him yet?"

"Uncle Bryan can't make it," Shelby said, appearing from behind him. "He called me and asked me to let you know. There's a plumbing issue in one of the cabins and he's dealing with that."

"I see." He noted that Shelby looked fresh and clear-eyed despite the early hour. Her blond curls were pulled into a loose ponytail, and she wore a pink-and-white-striped top with denim shorts. Far from his mental image of the typical accountant. And entirely too appealing, considering her father was standing three feet away watching them.

"If it's okay with you, I'll take Uncle Bryan's place in the boat," she said. "I just happen to know how to get to his secret fishing hole, and I guarantee you'll catch enough for your dinner tonight."

Though she spoke lightly, she gave him a significant look, proving once again that subtlety was not her strong suit. His lips twitching with a smile, he played his part, though flirting with her didn't exactly tax his limited acting skills. "No offense to your uncle, but you would definitely be my first choice for a fishing guide."

Her smile practically sparkled in approval. "Uncle Bryan is the real expert, but I know my way around the lake."

"Don't you have to work today?"

"Yes, but my hours are flexible. I can start later this morning."

"Then, by all means, let's fish."

Her father looked from one of them to the other, as if sensing a subtext he didn't quite understand, but Shelby rushed Aaron into a flat-bottomed fishing boat before her dad could ask any awkward questions. It was just as well Shelby had chosen accounting rather than investigation for a career, Aaron thought, fastening the mandatory life vest he'd been given to wear. Despite her penchant for elaborate schemes, she had little talent for subterfuge. And that was hardly a bad thing. The last woman he'd dated for any length of time had been able to lie without even blinking an eyelash.

"So, what did you do to the plumbing in the cabin?" he asked as Shelby threaded her ponytail through the back of a green ball cap emblazoned with the resort logo.

She frowned at him from beneath the bill, her expression delightfully indignant. "I didn't sabotage the plumbing! It was just a coincidence that it happened this morning when you had plans with Uncle Bryan."

He raised his hands in apology. "I was only teasing."

"Good." She started the motor with a jerk of the starter rope.

Aaron turned to face the front of the boat as she guided it out into the open water. Sliding his sunglasses onto his nose, he tugged his cap lower on his forehead to keep it from being blown off by the wind whipping past his cheeks. The front of the boat rose slightly out of the water, slapping against the surface as it sliced across the lake. The cushion beneath him softened his jarring against the aluminum seat.

Shelby guided the boat into one of the feeder creeks edging the large lake, the roar of the motor subsiding to a rumble as she circumvented underwater obstacles with the ease of familiarity. She stopped in a cove where the water glittered almost emerald in the morning sun. "You should catch some white bass in here, maybe a largemouth. We can go in a little closer to shore if you want to try for crappie or bream. I've caught plenty of pan-sized bluegills closer to that bank, but most guys seem to prefer catching bass."

Aaron chuckled. "I've got nothing against bream. Deep-fried and served with hush puppies and coleslaw, they're darned tasty."

She laughed and slipped on a pair of dark-rimmed sunglasses. "Yes, they are. Want to try for a bass first?"

"Sure." He opened his tackle box and drew out a three-inch crank bait. "This look about right?"

Examining his choice, she nodded. "Worth a try. Let's see your stuff, city boy."

They spent the next two hours casting, reeling, re- trieving snagged lures, occasionally landing a fish. They kept only a few, releasing the others back into the lake. Aaron admired Shelby's fishing skills, though he supposed they were only natural considering her background. Fortunately, he was practiced enough not to embarrass himself in front of her.

Shelby had brought two large travel mugs of coffee and Aaron sipped his as he watched her expertly land a lure in just the right spot to tempt a hungry fish. It was no surprise to him when she had an immediate strike. She reeled in a two-pound white bass, admired it for a moment, then thanked it for letting her catch it and released it back into the water.

Aaron grinned. In long-standing fisherman tradition, they hadn't talked a lot, preferring to savor the sounds of chattering birds and splashing fish, of water slapping against the banks and boat motors passing on the open lake. The silences hadn't been awkward, but pleasantly companionable. Occasionally, they pointed out things that caught their attention—a water snake gliding near the shore, a doe and her fawn cautiously taking a drink at the far end of the narrow cove, two big turtles sunning on a partially submerged log.

Lounging comfortably on his seat, he studied her through his tinted lenses. She looked relaxed, utterly at ease, completely genuine. If last night's kiss crossed her mind, she didn't let it show. She'd probably written it off as an impulsive action on his part for the benefit of Terrence Landon. Maybe she thought he was simply cooperating with the favor she had asked of him, that the kiss wasn't even worth mentioning today. She couldn't know how many times he had mentally replayed it after she'd left, brief though the embrace had been.

Once again he found himself remembering the last woman he'd been involved with. Elaina. Stunning, and fully aware of it. Clever, witty, seductive. Highly competent in her sales job, highly skilled in bed. She'd kept him so hot and bothered that it had taken him several months to realize there was almost nothing genuine about her. Everything she said and did had an agenda, every move she made was calculated and choreographed. Breaking up with her had probably been the impetus that had led him to reexamine his life yet again and determine that he hadn't been any happier in commercial real estate sales than he'd been in his tumultuous affair with Elaina.

Studying Shelby as she snapped a photo of a heron with her cell phone, he couldn't help but smile. There was no way Elaina would sit in a flat-bottomed fishing boat in denim shorts that revealed scratched knees, her hair escaping in damp tendrils from a battered ball cap, the smell of fish on her unpolished fingertips. Was Shelby really so unaware of her own appeal? She'd remarked so casually that her cousins and sister were the "pretty ones" in the family, as if she considered herself less attractive. He'd sensed that she hadn't been fishing for compliments, simply stating facts as she believed them.

In his opinion, she couldn't be more wrong. Maggie was certainly pretty, and he assumed Hannah was, too, though he hadn't seen her. Lori, though young, was definitely eye-catching, with her offbeat style and willowy figure. Yet Shelby was the one who brought a grin to his face, who could talk him into going along with her impulsive schemes and somehow make him think it was entirely rational, who had kept him awake for a good part of the night with the memory of a kiss she had yet to even acknowledge this morning. And he'd known her less than twenty-four hours. Which could be a sign that he needed to start being a lot more careful around her.

Slipping her phone back into her pocket, she gave him a quizzical look. "What?"

"Nothing. Just admiring the view."

Her smile pushed shallow dimples into her cheeks

beneath the rims of her big sunglasses. "You don't have to flirt with me now. No one's watching."

"Maybe I just need the practice."

She huffed out a skeptical laugh. "You? Yeah, right."

"Besides," he added, ignoring her implication that flirting came a bit too easily to him, "someone is watching us. Don't look around, but I think Terrence Landon is sitting in a boat just across the lake—I said don't turn around," he added quickly when she instinctively started to swivel on her seat.

She resisted but it was with an obvious effort. "Is he looking at us?" she asked in a loud whisper, though the other boater was too far away to hear a normal tone of voice.

"Occasionally. He's fishing, but you're right. He's not particularly good at it."

"Is he alone?"

"Yes."

"How long has he been there?"

"About fifteen minutes."

"And you're just now telling me?"

He chuckled quietly. "I was curious to see how long he would sit there. He doesn't seem to be in any hurry to leave."

"What should we do?"

He set his rod in the bottom of the boat. "What we'd have done even if he wasn't there. It's about time for you to get back to work, isn't it?"

"Yes," she admitted. "Have you fished enough?"

"I have. Want to join me for a fish fry this evening?"

"Oh, very clever," she said approvingly. "Yes, I'd like that."

She thought he was giving her an excuse to hang around his cabin again. Maybe he was—but it had little to do with spying on his neighbor. He just wanted to spend more time with her.

He reached out to tug at the brim of her cap, a gesture that was both teasing and flirtatious. Not nearly as satisfying as a kiss, but he would be seeing her later. "Then let's go. Give your guest a friendly wave when we pass him."

She did so—maybe a bit too energetically, but Aaron figured if the guy had spent any time at all around Shelby he'd have to know she did everything with enthusiasm. Following that line of thinking could lead him into trouble, he thought ruefully, lifting his chin in a casual greeting to the other fisherman.

Aaron was definitely attracted to Shelby, but that didn't necessarily mean he planned to do anything about it, other than to enjoy her company. Being surrounded by her extended family didn't exactly make a hot summer fling a likely possibility and he wasn't on the market for anything more. Even if this wasn't the worst time in his life to start a new relationship, Shelby had made it clear that she was happily ensconced here at the resort, and that she wasn't looking for anyone, either.

Which didn't mean he couldn't enjoy the time he spent with her, he thought, holding on to his cap as he sent her a grin over his shoulder. She beamed back at him, and he swallowed. Maybe another few kisses wouldn't be out of line…just for the sake of the favor she'd asked, of course.

Maggie set a stack of time sheets on the corner of Shelby's desk, then propped a hip on the desktop. "Warning—Lori's in a mood this morning."

Shelby groaned. Her sister's bad moods were notorious. Lori would speak pleasantly and professionally to any guests who crossed her path, but a hapless family member could end up with metaphorical bite marks. "Thanks. I'll keep a wide berth."

"We've talked her into taking some time off this afternoon. Mimi's going to run the front desk for a couple hours. So," Maggie added with an arch smile, "you took Aaron fishing this morning?"

A little startled by the abrupt change of subject, Shelby looked up from her computer keyboard and pushed back a curl that had escaped her ponytail to tickle her cheek. "Your dad invited him, but then Uncle Bryan had to deal with that plumbing problem in Cabin Four."

Maggie chuckled. "Yeah, the kid in there flushed a handful of rubber bath toys. They were shaped like sea creatures, so he thought they could swim through the pipes."

Laughing, Shelby shook her head. "I didn't hear that part."

"Dad said the kid's a terror. So about that fishing trip…"

Shelby lifted a shoulder. "After Uncle Bryan had to cancel, I volunteered to fill in. It's not like I've never taken a guest fishing before."

"Ah. So you were just being a good resort hostess."

"I didn't mind. You know I like to fish occasionally."

"Especially with a good-looking guy in the boat?"

"That does make a nice bonus," she admitted. "We had a pleasant outing. Aaron caught some fish and he invited me to join him for dinner this evening."

"Yeah? So…?"

"I said yes. But it's no big deal, Mags. I just met the guy yesterday."

"I know. But he did seem sort of taken with you,"

her cousin replied speculatively. "The way he looked at you yesterday—I don't remember his brother looking at you quite that way."

That comment pleased Shelby on several levels. It demonstrated the cover story she'd concocted was credible, so maybe Terrence Landon wouldn't question her spending extra time at the cabin next door. And she had to admit her ego was stroked by the prospect that her family would believe a man like Aaron would be interested in her. Ever since Pete had broken up with her, they'd been prone to reassuring her that there was someone out there who would appreciate her "unique qualities." Her pride had taken a beating from those well-intentioned encouragements. She wasn't even quite twenty-six yet, for heaven's sake!

Of course, considering that both she and Hannah had struck out big-time when it came to romance—Hannah almost taking the rest of the family down with her— and that neither of her siblings nor Maggie had thus far found a compatible match, maybe her generation just didn't have the same luck with love their parents and grandparents had experienced.

"Aaron's a nice guy," she said lightly. "I find it interesting how different he is from his brother, even though they're identical in appearance. If he wants a little company while he's here, I certainly don't mind spending time with him."

Maggie frowned and searched her face. "Okay, what's going on?"

Shelby widened her eyes. "I don't know what you mean."

"Right. This is about the guy in Cabin Seven, isn't it? You've roped Aaron into investigating him."

Shelby sighed. She'd been trying to convince her

family for more than a week that something strange
was going on in Cabin Seven and no one had taken her
concerns seriously. But everyone sure seemed interested in what was going on with her and the occupant
of Cabin Eight. "I haven't roped Aaron into anything."

"But you asked him to look into it?"

"Maybe," she muttered. "He still invited me to have
dinner with him. His idea, not mine."

"Right. " Maggie nodded as though a question had
just been answered for her. She straightened away from
the desk. "Now I understand. Okay, have fun playing
detective with the hot twin. Just try to stay out of trouble, okay? Hannah's got enough issues for the lot of us."

Thinking of her other cousin's current situation,
Shelby nodded grimly. "I'll see you later, Maggie."

So maybe her cover story wasn't quite so foolproof,
after all, she thought when Maggie left her office. So
far both her mother and her cousin had almost instantly guessed that she'd asked Aaron to spy on Terrence Landon. And Maggie hadn't seemed to think it
likely that Aaron had met Shelby yesterday and been
instantly attracted to her. Which wasn't particularly
flattering, but not really a surprise, either, she thought
pragmatically.

"You're a great girl," Pete had told her the night
they'd had their breakup talk. "One of the best pals
I've ever had, you know? But the thing is—well, I guess
I'm not looking for a pal as a girlfriend."

She hadn't even gotten mad at him for saying it—
other than wishing she'd been the one to say it first—
because she'd felt much the same way. Pete was a nice
guy, fun to be with, nice-looking in an average way—
but she'd been aware that something was missing in
their relationship. She'd been considering breaking it off

herself, but he'd beaten her to it. Which meant no one had believed she wasn't really heartbroken. They simply assumed that when she said she'd planned to break up with Pete, she was bravely saving face.

She sighed and reached for the computer mouse. The thing was, she'd learned how to cast before she could write, could clean a fish blindfolded, could back up a boat trailer into a space barely wide enough to clear the tires, could jump a ramp on water skis and spin around in midair before landing on the water again, could keep the books balanced and taxes in order…but she had never mastered the simple art of flirtation. She was just as likely to get the giggles if she tried being vampy, was more prone to sprint than slink, and tended to rattle off whatever thoughts crossed her mind rather than carefully choosing words designed to appeal to a man's ego.

She knew Aaron was entertained by her. He seemed to like her. But as for anything more, she had asked him to play a part and he was going along with her, either as a favor to his brother's friend or because it amused him to do so. Maybe a little of both. He'd kissed her, but only because Landon was watching them. Not that he'd seemed to mind. He had probably even enjoyed the experience. Whereas she'd been so stunned she'd had to concentrate fiercely on driving the half mile to her home without running into trees.

Shaking her head in self-recrimination, she focused on her computer monitor, reminding herself that she had work to do.

Aaron cleaned his catch, stashed the filets in the fridge, put away his gear and then checked his watch. Not even quite noon on his second day of vacation.

With a wry smile, he glanced at the resort brochure

on the kitchen bar, the flyer he'd found on Andrew's office floor. The colorful photos weren't misleading. So far this morning, he'd seen people fishing, swimming, boating, biking—all the activities shown in the ad. Maybe he'd had vague ideas of throwing himself into that action when he'd impulsively headed this way, but he wasn't really in the mood for any of it at the moment. If Shelby had been free to play with him, he was sure he'd have enjoyed any of those pursuits, but she had to work. Unlike her obviously boneheaded ex, Aaron admired rather than resented that she took her responsibilities to the family business seriously.

He had several hours to kill before Shelby joined him for dinner. He could call home, but he wasn't in any hurry to listen to more of his mom's fretting or his dad's lectures. Maybe because of his own painful and unsettled past, Ryan Walker was convinced that his sons should be settled down and career-focused.

Aaron knew he needed to start job hunting. He'd even thought about going back to school, training for a new career, getting a more specific focus than the general business degree he'd already earned. He had cousins who were doctors, lawyers, teachers, cops, even a professional poker player. There were plenty of choices open to him. As long as it wasn't doing endless computer searches or boring stakeouts for Dee-Dub. Andrew might love that life, but it wasn't for him.

He should drive into town for a few extra supplies for the fish dinner he would serve to Shelby later, but he had plenty of time for that. He decided to walk around the resort for a while, instead. It wasn't yet too hot for a long walk, and he wanted to get a good look at the place.

If his neighbor had returned from his fishing outing, Aaron saw no sign of the guy when he dutifully glanced that way upon heading out. Directly opposite his cabin, a road led through two parallel rows of RV pads before joining the main road that circled around to the exit on the far side. He turned right instead, taking the main road in the opposite direction of the marina. RV pads lined the riverbank on his right, between him and the glittering water, and most were occupied even on this Wednesday morning. The occupants ranged from pickup-mounted camper shells to hydraulics-expanded motor homes that probably had more living space than his apartment in Dallas. Small vehicles that had been pulled behind the RVs sat in the parking spaces, and he spotted quite a few bicycles and scooters. Vacationers visited in folding chairs or puttered around their campsites laying out lunches while children played noisily and sullen teens hunched with their cell phones and headphones.

He paused to study the tent-camping area. Okay, this was more his style, he thought. Shelters ranging from one-man pup tents to multiroom family tents were arranged beneath large, shady trees. Strings of multicolored plastic lights in whimsical shapes hung from tree branches, and folding chairs were grouped for conversation around fire pits. Additional RV pads lay beyond the tent area, and because they were farther from the water, more of them were vacant. He imagined that would change as the weekend grew closer.

Having walked halfway around the circumference of the resort, he came to a road marked with a private-drive sign. This, he would bet, would lead to the homes of the Bell family. Through a heavy stand of trees, he could see glimpses of houses. During their fishing outing that morning, Shelby had mentioned that she and her brother and cousins lived in manufactured homes in a private lot near their parents. He was tempted to explore, just for curiosity, but decided the family's hospitality did not extend to trespassing.

A green utility ATV buzzed up behind him, the driver a sandy-haired man in his twenties. Tall and fit-looking, muscles work-hardened rather than gym-toned, he wore a resort-logo cap and polo shirt with khaki shorts, and looked enough like C.J. and Shelby that Aaron had little trouble identifying him.

"Wow." Stopping the vehicle, Steven Bell pushed his cap back on his head with his thumb to give him a better look at Aaron. "They warned me, but I've got to admit it's still a shock how much you look like Andrew."

"You must be Steven. I'm Aaron."

"Yeah, I figured." Steven leaned out to shake Aaron's hand. "Nice to meet you."

"You, too."

"Checking out the resort?"

"Yes. Great place."

"I was just headed to the utility shed to get a saw and a stepladder. I noticed a dead limb dangling over one of the sites earlier and thought I would take it down before it falls. If you want to ride along, I'll show you around the family compound."

"Hey, I'd like that. Thanks." Aaron rounded the cart to climb into the passenger seat.

The family compound, as Steven had referred to it, was tidy and inviting. The three main houses were similar, redbrick ranch-style homes with white trim and shutters and covered front porches. The grounds were immaculate, flower beds blooming, lawns shaded by tall trees. The road ended in a turnaround with two mobile homes positioned on either side.

"We call this the trailer park," Steven said with a

chuckle, waving toward those manufactured homes. "That's where my generation lives for now, though there's room for two or three more traditional houses in line with the folks' places."

Aaron noted that the mobile homes were quality structures with brick underpinning and redwood decking. All were in variations of tan and cream, which gave them a consistent appearance. Shrubs and flowers in beds around each home softened the angular lines and added to the welcoming atmosphere. The trees here were smaller, having been planted after the units were hauled in, but would provide nice shade in a couple more years.

A big, lazy-looking yellow lab ambled up to the vehicle. Steven stopped to rub the dog's ears. "This is Pax. I've had him for almost seven years."

"Hey, Pax, how's it going?"

The lab wagged his tail.

"I bought the first trailer," Steven said, pointing to the first house on the left. "Took me a while to convince Pop that bringing in a mobile home wouldn't ruin the family compound. Then Maggie decided she'd like her own quarters, and she put in the one opposite mine on your right. Hannah moved in next to Maggie after her divorce, and Shelby bought the one next to me when she finished college."

"Sounds like you started a trend."

"Much to Pop's annoyance. He'd still rather we'd build houses. But I just turned twenty-seven last month, you know? I'm not ready to pore over blueprints and choose countertops and paint colors. Hannah might think about building in a year or two, but the rest of us are okay with what we've got for now."

Aaron wasn't at all sure Steven was satisfied, in any

way. Maybe he was projecting, but he thought he recognized a fellow restless soul. Shelby had hinted that her brother felt somewhat stifled here. Which wouldn't be at all surprising. Experimenter that he'd been, Aaron couldn't imagine spending his entire life living within sight of his parents, grandparents, siblings and cousins, his whole future mapped out for him. "Shelby said you assist Bryan in groundskeeping."

"Yeah." The lack of enthusiasm in the other man's voice only confirmed Aaron's suspicion.

Maybe Steven sensed his answer had lacked something. Sending Pax back to his napping place, he turned the ATV around in the cul-de-sac, then drove past the houses again. "I was the envy of a lot of my friends, growing up in a fishing and camping resort. Some of them still think I fish and ski all day. They have no idea how much work goes into a place like this. We've been fortunate that the bad economy hasn't taken too hard a hit on us, though it helps that there's enough family to keep it running with a minimum of outside help."

And there, Aaron thought, was the key to why Steven didn't feel free to leave. Just as Shelby had implied, Steven took his obligation to the family business seriously enough to feel shackled by it, whether or not he actually enjoyed the work. Aaron would have felt the same way had his dad roped him into working for the agency his entire life. Fortunately, D'Alessandro-Walker was not dependent solely on family to keep the company running. The long-established security and investigation business was profitable and stable, and had more than enough job applicants from a pool of computer whizzes and law-enforcement types.

Steven stopped the cart at a wood-sided utility building behind his parents' house. The building blended so well into the landscaping that it didn't detract from the view, even though it was large and designed for function. When Steven opened one of the heavily padlocked doors, Aaron could see mowing and other maintenance equipment along with an assortment of power tools and supplies. Steven threw a four-foot stepladder and a gas-powered pole saw into the open bed of the utility vehicle, then climbed back behind the wheel. "Want a ride back to your cabin? You're in Cabin Eight, aren't you?"

"I am, but if you don't mind, I'd like to ride along and watch you take down the limb. I can help, if you need me. I find the behind-the-scenes operations of a resort interesting."

Steven chuckled. "Most of our guests prefer enjoying the lake or other amenities we offer, but sure, you're welcome to watch me cut a limb."

Aaron grinned. "I guess there's no accounting for what some people find fun."

Steven could have figured out a way to accomplish the task alone, but Aaron believed his help made the job easier. The sizable limb dangled more than twelve feet up in a tree near a currently unoccupied tent pad. While it was unlikely that it would have fallen on a hapless camper protected by no more than a canvas roof, Aaron agreed that it was best to make sure. Maybe Steven was fighting restlessness, but he was still conscientious about his work.

Standing on top of the ladder with the pole saw extended to its full reach, Steven cut through the narrow part of the limb still attached to the trunk while Aaron steadied him and kept an eye on the limb's trajectory when it came down. It caught on several other limbs on the way, but Steven was able to guide it with the tip of the saw until Aaron could grab hold of the branch and tug it down to the ground, jumping out of the way when it landed with a cloud of dirt and dried leaves.

"Thanks, Aaron," Steven said, climbing down from the ladder and wiping his forehead with the back of one hand. "I appreciate the help."

"No problem. Nice-sized limb for firewood."

Steven nodded and started the saw again to cut the limb into manageable lengths. Aaron stacked the fire-pit-sized results in the bed of the utility vehicle. They chatted about fishing and hiking while they cleared away the debris. It turned out they shared a fondness for mountain hiking when they were able to get away from work. Steven had friends in Colorado whom he joined a couple times a year, while Aaron was more likely to head for the Smoky Mountains in east Tennessee, where his cousins Casey and Molly had settled with their spouses.

"I've never been to the Gatlinburg area," Steven admitted.

"Some of the prettiest countryside I've seen, and I've been all over the States. There's something like eight hundred miles of hiking trails in the national park alone. My cousin Molly married a guy who co-owns and manages vacation rental cabins around Gatlinburg. Sort of like your line of work, except his rentals are scattered through the area rather than located on a resort like this."

"You've traveled a lot, huh?" A note of what might have been envy underscored Steven's question.

Aaron shrugged. "Some. Mostly in the lower forty-eight."

"I'm lucky to have a week off every few months to visit my friends in Colorado. This place is pretty much twenty-four-seven, year-round."

Brushing bits of bark from his hands, Aaron asked casually, "So if you didn't work here, what do you think you'd be doing?"

Steven tossed the saw into the ATV and laid the ladder on top of the wood. He shrugged, then said rather sheepishly, "Oh, you know. I had the typical boyhood aspirations. Always thought I wanted to be a fireman. Well, specifically a forest firefighter. I think I'd have done that if I hadn't been needed here. My folks always encouraged us to do what we wanted—but Mom turned pale every time I even mentioned an interest in smoke jumping. Then I got busy helping around here, and before I knew it, the years were passing. Don't get me wrong, this is a good life. I'm crazy about my family. But you asked what I'd do if I wasn't working here."

Aaron had to admit he was surprised by Steven's response to his question. Despite the qualifications, the answer hadn't been impulsive. Steven had given a lot of thought to that abandoned dream. "You're definitely still young enough to train for firefighting," he said as he climbed back into the passenger seat. "You're obviously in good physical condition, and you know your way around saws and shovels. I'd imagine you'd be hired immediately."

"Yeah, well, that's not going to happen." Steven started the motor and drove onto the roadway, giving a friendly wave to some guests who'd been watching them work from a nearby campsite. "Like I said, boyhood dream. You probably had a few yourself."

"A few." And he'd experimented with several of them. Turned out they'd been better as dreams than reality. But at least he'd had the freedom to try them.

Steven parked in front of Cabin Eight. Aaron glanced instinctively toward the cabin next door. An expensive red sports car sat in the drive, next to the dark SUV that had been parked there since he'd arrived, which he assumed belonged to Terrence Landon. Steven followed his glance. "Haven't seen that car before," he commented. "The guy sure has a lot of company. Associates, he says."

"So Shelby told me."

Shelby's brother chuckled dryly. "Yeah, we figured she's got you checking him out. She's been suspicious of him since he checked in."

"I heard. I haven't seen anything particularly bothersome, though I've been here less than a day."

Steven hesitated a moment, then grimaced. "As much as I hate to give credence to one of Shelby's unlikely theories, I have to concede the guy is strange. He won't let the housekeeping staff in, just meets them at the door for clean linens. He says he's OCD about having people touching his things, despite his parade of guests. Last week when we were working on the cabin you're staying in, he kept spying on us through his blinds, like he suspected we were up to something besides our jobs. If he really is up to no good in there, he's not exactly being smart about it."

"Yeah, well, most criminals aren't known for their intelligence. But could be he's just weird."

"I forgot to ask what you do when you aren't on vacation. If you call helping with groundskeeping vacation," Steven added with a grin. "Are you a P.I. like your brother, or do you focus on the security side of the firm? Andrew told us corporate security is the major emphasis of your business, with private investigation being secondary."

"Actually, I'm between jobs, trying to decide what I want to do next," Aaron confessed. "I haven't mentioned that to Shelby. She seems to think just being Andrew's brother qualifies me to figure out what's going on in Cabin Seven."

"Kind of hard to tell her no, isn't it?"

Aaron laughed. "Yeah. It is. But I like her."

"Don't tell her I said so, but so do I."

Aaron slid out of the ATV. "See you around, Steven."

"Sure. Maybe we can take a couple of Jet Skis out tomorrow. I'll have some free time tomorrow afternoon."

The family certainly had been hospitable, Aaron thought, wondering again if they were like this with everyone or if their seemingly oversized gratitude toward Andrew influenced them toward him. "I'll look forward to it."

"So, uh—"

Having turned toward the cabin, Aaron paused to look over his shoulder. "Something else?"

"I was just thinking about what you said. About trying to decide what job to do next. No parental pressure, huh?"

Aaron had to laugh. "Trust me, there's plenty of that—from my parents and my brother. Not to join the family firm, necessarily, but to do something productive and worthwhile. And to stick with it."

Draping an arm over the steering wheel, Steven asked, "No boyhood dreams you still want to pursue?"

"That's what I'm here to think about."

Steven nodded and pulled his cap lower over his forehead. "We'll make sure you have a good time while you're thinking."

"I have no doubt of that."

Aaron watched Steven drive off. Like Shelby, he seemed to be open and gregarious. Whatever career frustrations he suffered, he was more pragmatic than bitter. He'd admitted it was his choice to stay here, though it was obvious he felt the burden of obligation. Maybe it weighed more heavily on him as the only male in his generation. He'd seemed to enjoy having another guy close to his age to talk with for a little while.

He turned to his cabin, digging in his pocket for the key. Just as he reached the porch, Terrence Landon and another man, this one middle-aged and a little doughy, stepped out next door. Both of them looked hard at Aaron, then the older man hurried to the sports car, a couple of cardboard boxes in his arms. He threw the boxes in the passenger seat of his car and drove off without looking back. Landon slammed his door and Aaron could hear the click of the lock from where he stood.

The guy really was weird, he thought with a shake of his head. Didn't mean he was concocting evil plots over there, of course, but he could see why Shelby's suspicions had been raised. Speaking of Shelby...

He glanced at his watch. He had time to wash up and head to town for dinner supplies, after which he'd start cooking for his guest. Maybe she was just coming over to spy on his neighbor, but Aaron found himself looking forward to the evening a bit too eagerly. Especially since he'd been telling himself that nothing significant was going to happen between them. Somehow, that didn't seem to dim his enthusiasm.

An hour later, he stashed his grocery purchases in the backseat of his car, pleased by the selection he'd found at the modest-sized supermarket he'd happened upon not far from the resort. A small coffee shop with a recognizable logo shared the parking lot with the grocery store. It was too warm for a hot beverage, but an iced mocha to go sounded good for the short drive back to the cabin.

Deciding the groceries would be fine for the couple minutes it took him to run in and place his order, he locked the car and went inside. The lighting was dim, the air conditioner blasting to provide a chilly contrast to the summer heat. Folksy guitar music played from hidden speakers, and the aroma of brewing coffee wafted temptingly from behind the counter, upon which a tempting display of pastries was arranged in a glass case. He hadn't thought of dessert for tonight, he realized. He wasn't much of a baker, so he ordered a couple of sugar-dusted lemon bars along with his iced coffee.

After paying the flirty barista, he turned toward the door with his purchases, only to stop when he recognized the young woman sitting in the darkest corner of the shop. Lori Bell wasn't alone—and she wasn't exactly sitting. Rather, she was wound around a long-haired, bearded guy in a black tee and black jeans, their lips fused in a kiss that would have been more fittingly exchanged in private.

She must have spotted him out of the corner of her eye. Peeling herself away from the embrace, she looked shocked to see him. He nodded in greeting. "Hello, Lori."

Murmuring something to her friend, she stood and hurried toward him, her filmy gray sundress fluttering around her. She seemed to dress in shades of mist, he thought. Not as clichéd as her companion's stark black, but definitely a statement of its own, especially when combined with her black-and-blue hair.

"Um—hi, Aaron," she said, her smile strained. "I didn't expect to see you here."

He held up his bag of pastries. "Just picking up a few groceries and snacks. Taking a little time off, yourself?"

She nodded somberly. "Listen, Aaron, I'd really appreciate it if you don't mention seeing me here, especially with—"

She looked toward the young man watching them with a grim expression. "My family hates him," she confided with a sigh. "They would freak if they knew about...well, what you just saw."

"I see no reason to mention running into you," he assured her. Lori was over eighteen. It was certainly none of his business whom she wanted to make out with in a public coffee shop, though that didn't seem the brightest location in which to carry on a secret romance.

Gratitude flooded her pretty, dramatically made-up face. She rested a silver-nailed hand on his arm for a moment. "Thank you."

He shrugged. "Sure. I'll see you around. Uh—take care," he added, the closest to a warning he felt acceptable to offer her.

Her smile glittered, a hint of a hard edge making her look older than her years. "Sure, no problem. See you, Aaron."

Shaking his head in bemusement, he headed for his car, needing to get his groceries put away as soon as possible. He thought about the promise Lori had just elicited from him. Yet another confidence shared with him by one of the Bell siblings, though this one had been by accident.

Hard to believe he'd known this family less than twenty-four hours, he thought with a rueful chuckle. And even though he'd come here to escape the hovering of family, he found himself surrounded by yet another too-close clan. The irony did not escape him.

Chapter Five

Shelby spent entirely too much time thinking about what she was going to wear for dinner with Aaron. For someone who usually cared so little about fashion, especially for a casual fish fry in the resort, she had a hard time making up her mind. She even thought about asking Maggie's advice, but she rejected that impulse immediately, telling herself not to be ridiculous. After taking a shower, she donned a pair of jeans and a white top with lace edging and tiny buttons running down the front. Feminine, a little dressier than work clothes, but not over the top for a fish fry, she decided. She brushed on a touch of makeup, left her hair loose and curly and decided that was enough primping.

Aaron had instructed her not to bring anything, but that didn't seem right. She wasn't much of a baker, as her family could attest, but her specialty was a quickie peanut butter cookie with chocolate chips. If Aaron had provided another dessert for this evening, she would leave the cookies with him for snacks. She figured everyone liked peanut butter cookies. Unless they were allergic to peanuts, she thought with a sudden frown, clutching the plastic container of cookies in her hands. She'd made the cookies once when Andrew was here, and he hadn't been allergic. Could one identical twin be allergic to peanuts and not the other?

Sighing, she shoved her keys into her pocket and moved toward the door. If Aaron was allergic, he would surely tell her rather than risk death to be polite. Why was she overthinking everything this evening?

She decided to ride her bike rather than walk or take a golf cart. Snapping her hot-pink-and-purple helmet on her head, she pedaled past the family houses and toward Cabin Eight, taking the most direct path past the tent area. The familiar smells of smoldering charcoal briquettes and grilling meats wafted past her as campers prepared their evening meals. Some cooked inside their fancy RVs, and others went into town or to the Chimes Grill for dinner, but outdoor grilling was as much a part of camping as water sports. She exchanged waves and nods with people she passed, then swerved to miss a yappy little dog who'd escaped its pursuing owner. There was a strict leash rule in the resort, but Shelby didn't bother to remind the obviously embarrassed owner, who held a dangling leash in her hand as she scooped up the mischievous pup.

She saw Aaron moving around outside his cabin before she pedaled into the driveway. She skidded to a stop, put down the kickstand and reached up slowly to unfasten her helmet without taking her eyes off Aaron. How foolish was she to think he was even better-looking than his twin? The man was pure perfection in jeans and a pale yellow polo shirt that emphasized the rich tan of skin and coffee-brown of hair and eyes. Had she really asked him to allow her to reject him in front of her family? Sometimes she amazed herself with her own crazy impulses. As for why he'd agreed—apparently he was easily amused.

She saw that he'd set the picnic table, using a red-and-white-checked plastic cloth and bright blue unbreakable plates from the cabin's kitchen. She did not recognize the cheery yellow vase holding a bouquet of white daisies at the center of the table. A fat citronella candle in a clear glass holder flickered beside the daisies. Even though the sun had not yet set, the candle added a nice touch. That wasn't something they provided, either. Aaron had been shopping.

He turned to smile at her in greeting and her pulse rate tripped in response. She reminded herself not to take any of this too seriously. So maybe she didn't remember her heart ever doing quite this same frantic Texas two-step just because a good-looking man smiled at her. Maybe she found herself getting mesmerized by those gleaming dark eyes to a point where she, who rarely lacked for words, could hardly put a coherent sentence together. And maybe the fact that he'd set out daisies and a candle made her knees go all shaky. It was all just an act, at least on his part.

She brushed a hand through her hair to make sure it hadn't been flattened by the helmet she'd left dangling from her handlebars. "Everything looks very nice," she said, carrying the container of cookies as she approached him. "I hope you didn't go to too much trouble."

"I had a good time with it," he assured her. "It's been a while since I put together a fish fry."

"What can I do to help?"

"Everything's ready."

She raised her eyebrows in surprise. She'd assumed she would be helping him prepare the meal. "Oh—well."

A little flustered, she all but shoved the plastic container into his hands. "I made some cookies. If you've prepared another dessert, you can save these for later."

"Actually, I don't really make desserts. I just bought some lemon bars. We'll have both." He set the container on the table. "Have a seat. I'll bring out the food."

They couldn't see Cabin Seven from this side of Aaron's cabin, and trees blocked sight of the first RV pad on the other side, so they were able to enjoy the meal in a semblance of outdoor privacy. They were visible from the road and the lake, of course, but Shelby had lived so much of her life surrounded by resort guests that she hardly noted passersby while she and Aaron ate and chatted.

"This is really good," she complimented him halfway through the meal. He had fried the fish fillets in a crisp breading and had made his own tartar sauce and crunchy, tart coleslaw. Rather than fries, he served oven-roasted potato wedges and yellow pepper slices tossed with olive oil and rosemary. "I'm impressed."

Though he looked pleased, he shrugged lightly. "I'm sure you get tired of fried fish, living in a resort all your life."

"You changed it up. The spices on the fish are delicious."

"I added a few Cajun seasonings. Not too spicy, I hope."

"No, I love everything spicy."

He winked at her. "So do I."

Shelby cleared her throat. "Um, the coleslaw is really different, too."

"Jicama, green apples, red onion and carrots tossed with a little low-fat mayo, lemon juice and rice wine vinegar. A little salt and pepper. Easy."

"And healthy. Actually, the whole meal is pretty healthy, considering the main course is fried."

"I fried the fillets in canola oil and drained them as well as I could, but some foods just cry out to be deep-fried. Like fresh-caught fish," he added with a chuckle. "My mom's a health-food nut. Andrew and I were raised on fresh fruits and veggies and lean, broiled or grilled meats. Our favorite after-school snack was a ball of equal parts peanut butter and oatmeal, kept firm in the fridge. Sometimes she'd stir in some raisins or carob chips."

At least she knew now that he wasn't allergic to peanuts. "My mom tried to raise us on healthy food, but it wasn't easy living here at the resort," she confessed. "With her running the grill every day and so much fried food and convenience-store snacks all around us, it was hard not to fall into bad food habits."

"You all look healthy enough."

She laughed ruefully. "It's not that difficult to stay in pretty good shape with the amount of physical activity that goes into running a resort this size. Even keeping the books, I'm always walking or biking or skiing or swimming. I'm too restless to sit still for very long."

Maybe it was just an automatic response that his gaze swept her body from head to toe. He looked back at his plate quickly, but still her skin tingled as though there had been actual physical contact between them. *Stop this right now, Shelby.*

"I met your brother today," he said.

Grateful for the change of subject, she nodded. "I heard. He said you helped him cut down a dead limb."

"Yeah. I just happened to be walking past at the time. Nice guy."

"He likes you, too. He said you're going out on the water tomorrow."

"Yes. Want to join us?"

"Maybe I will," she said, pleased that he'd asked, even if it was simply to further their cover story.

Speaking of which… "Steven told me your neighbor had another visitor today," she said in a stage whisper.

"He did. But I'm afraid I didn't notice any contraband changing hands between them."

He'd spoken teasingly, but he wasn't mocking her. She knew the difference all too well. "You know, there probably is nothing illegal going on over there," she admitted. "The guy's odd, but that's hardly against the law."

Aaron laughed. "If it was, half my family would be locked up. Myself included, I guess."

Grinning, she shook her head. "You've met the Bells, right? I think we could give the Walkers a run for your money."

He took a sip of the light beer he'd been nursing during his meal. "You might be surprised."

"Do you and Andrew have any other siblings?" She knew very little about their family, actually. She hadn't realized quite how little Andrew had shared until she'd discovered there was an identical twin he'd never even mentioned.

"No. Dad said the two of us were all they could handle."

She giggled, remembering the "terrible trio" nickname they and their cousin had been given. "You said your dad is a twin, too?"

He nodded. "Also identical. The only way you can tell them apart is that my father has a scar across his left eyebrow."

"How do people tell you and Andrew apart?"

He flashed a smile. "I'm the better-looking one."

She wrinkled her nose at him, even though she foolishly agreed with the joking comment.

Shaking his head, he said, "No, really, people who know us well rarely get us mixed up. I mean, there's the hair—Andrew has always liked his shorter—and just something about our personalities, I guess, that tips them off."

She could understand that. She was quite different from her own siblings, of course, but she'd never really thought about identical twins having such diverse personalities. She'd bet that was frustrating for twins trying hard to establish their own unique identities.

The shadows around them had lengthened as the sun dropped lower, glittering golden on the water, deepening the sky to azure. She hardly noticed the sounds of boat motors and drifting conversation and laughter and children's chatter, a few barking dogs and the rumble of a passing motorbike. Any out-of-the-ordinary sound would catch her attention, but this was simply the everyday background of her life.

What made up the soundtrack of Aaron's life in Dallas? Traffic, car horns, sirens? Did he live in the city or the suburbs? There was so much she found herself eager to know about him. "What was it like growing up in a family of private investigators?" she asked, propping her elbows on the picnic table to study him.

He seemed to find her wording funny. "My dad's not

much different than any other businessman. He goes to the office every day carrying a briefcase, comes home most evenings in time for dinner. He and my uncles gave up stakeouts and most out-of-town trips years ago, focusing on the management of the business instead. Dad said he got tired of being shot at and living undercover identities. After he was a married man with kids, he said he found all the adventure and excitement he needed at home with us."

"That's nice. But—he was shot at?" she asked with a puzzled tilt of her head. "Andrew told me the investigation business is a lot less dangerous than fiction would have us believe."

"That's true," Aaron acknowledged. "But most of my dad's escapades took place before the D'Alessandro-Walker Agency was even formed. He and my uncle Joe worked in risky undercover government operations for a while when they were younger. They also served as bodyguards in a few dangerous situations. They don't tell us a lot of the details, but we've figured out that their lives were on the line more than once."

"Wow."

"Uncle Joe actually met his wife, my aunt Lauren, when he was working as her bodyguard. Her dad was a judge in an organized-crime case and Lauren was seen as a threat to hold over his head. My uncle was shot protecting her, almost died, himself."

"Oh, my gosh! Was your dad hurt, too?"

"He wasn't involved in that operation. Dad was nearly killed a couple years earlier than that when he was deliberately run down by a speeding car on an undercover operation in the Caribbean. To this day, he has no memory of that incident—which means he doesn't remember meeting my mother."

She must have looked thoroughly bewildered. Aaron laughed and explained. "Dad met my mother during that operation. She was a photographer on a photo shoot, totally unconnected to his investigation, but they crossed paths at the worst possible time for him. Because of the sensitive and dangerous nature of his investigation, and because he and my mom had just met and she was deemed a possible security risk, she was told he died of his injuries. She says it broke her heart. Two years later, they ran into each other again in Dallas when Dad and his twin tracked down their long-lost biological sister, who was my mom's best friend. Dad didn't have a clue who Mom was, but she recognized him as the lover who had supposedly died in front of her, which—needless to say—was awkward all around. They fell in love all over again, married and had us, so it all worked out."

Shelby followed along with an effort. "Your dad fell in love with his long-lost sister's best friend while he was undercover in the Caribbean?"

Aaron's chuckle was wry, as if he fully understood her confusion. "Yes. Then found her again two years later. Trust me, we know how improbable it seems. One of my cousins is really into fate and the stars and stuff like that, and she's convinced paths are meant to cross. She insists that when Mom and Dad were separated through no fault of their own, fate stepped in to bring them back together."

Sighing, Shelby murmured, "That's so romantic."

"I can't dispute that they were meant to be together. Even all these years later, my folks are crazy about each other."

"Is your mom still best friends with your dad's sister?"

"Oh, sure. Mom and Aunt Michelle are as close as

sisters themselves. Michelle's husband, Tony, is the
D'Alessandro part of D'Alessandro-Walker. He was already a P.I. when my dad and Uncle Joe were reunited
with Michelle. When he heard about their undercover
work, he talked them into joining and expanding his
own fledgling agency."

"You have a very interesting family history."

He wiped his hands on a paper napkin and grinned.
"You've only heard part of it. Dad and his twin were
separated from five other siblings when they were still
in kindergarten, after their parents died. Two of them
were adopted, the others went into foster care. One died
in his late teens, leaving a pregnant girlfriend behind.
Almost thirty-five years ago, my aunt Michelle hired
Tony to find her siblings. That's how Michelle and Tony
met. Anyway, the siblings were all reunited—they even
found the daughter their late brother left behind—and
they've remained very close since. We get together often
so that I've grown up close to my cousins. Pretty much
like you and Maggie and Hannah. We don't all live in
the same compound the way you do, but it seems like
we're always gathering for some family event or another."

In only one dinnertime conversation, she had learned
more about the Walker family than in the almost two
weeks she'd known Andrew last year. And she found
it fascinating. "No wonder Andrew considers private
investigation to be an average, everyday-type career.
With your family history, adventure and the unexpected
are just ordinary occurrences!"

"Yeah," he conceded. "Our background is a little offbeat. But you have to admit yours isn't all that average,
either. Not everyone grows up in a resort."

"That's true. I'm not complaining about my life—it's

been great. I don't really want to do anything else. But I can see how some people would think it's too restrictive and stifling." Pete, for example.

"Like your ex?" Aaron asked, eerily echoing her thought.

She shrugged. "I guess you understand. Since you work for your family, too."

He cleared his throat. "Um—actually, I don't work for the agency."

"You don't?"

"No." Taking a deep breath, as though he wasn't quite sure how she would respond, he gave her a succinct summary of his current state of unemployment. "I was doing pretty well in commercial real estate, but I hated it," he concluded. "I figure there's got to be something better suited to me, even if I haven't found it yet."

"Oh."

"But I'm still keeping an eye on you-know-who for you," he assured her with a glance in the direction of Cabin Seven. "And I've got Andrew looking into him. To a point, of course. We're skirting the line as it is without more to go on than your feeling that something is hinky."

She nodded slowly. "I know. Like I said, it was just a hunch. I wouldn't want to get you or Andrew into any trouble. So, you aren't going to work for the agency now?"

"No." As uncertain as he'd been about his next career pursuit, he sounded adamant enough on that point. "Working for family just isn't my thing. Way too many people around who feel free to observe and comment on everything I do."

She wondered if Aaron's confession explained some of the tension she'd sensed between him and Andrew.

Was Andrew pressuring Aaron to work for the agency? Or otherwise criticizing his brother's choices? She wouldn't ask, of course, but she was definitely curious.

As if he'd grown tired of this line of conversation, Aaron started gathering the remains of their dinner. "How about a walk along the riverbank to work off our dinner before we dive into dessert?"

She rose with a smile, pushing any more questions to the back of her mind. "That sounds nice."

Aaron held out his hand to her and she hesitated only a split second before placing hers into it.

Just playing his part, she reminded herself as his long fingers curled warmly around hers. And he certainly played it well.

Daylight was fading, clouds beginning to gather in preparation for the rain that was predicted for later that night. But for now it was dry and comfortable, with a steady breeze from the emptying lake. Aaron could feel the promise of rain in the air. Still holding Shelby's hand in his right, he pushed his left hand through his wind-tossed hair, picking his way carefully down the rocky bank from the cabin to the water. Waves generated by a passing motorboat lapped lightly against the shore, licking at the soles of his sneakers.

Shelby turned her face to the breeze, not even trying to restrain the curls that danced around her shoulders. "It's getting cooler," she murmured.

"Wind's blowing the rain this way."

"We can use the rain. It keeps the fire risk down."

He chuckled. "As long as it's not stormy. A light rain isn't bad when you're sleeping in a tent, but it can get pretty damp in a downpour."

"That sounds like the voice of experience."

"I've spent a few soggy nights shivering in a wet sleeping bag."

"Even though I've lived my entire life here in the resort, I don't think I've ever spent the night in a wet sleeping bag. Sounds miserable."

"Oh, I usually managed to have a good time, anyway."

"I'll just bet you did," Shelby murmured.

He winked at her. Unbidden, an image came to his mind—himself snuggled in a tent with Shelby while rain fell gently on the canvas above them. Flickering lantern light would play beautifully over her pretty face, and bring out the gold in her blond curls. Her tanned shoulders would gleam softly—as would the rest of her when he took his time exploring every inch.

She wiggled her fingers in his. "Ouch."

Immediately he loosened his grip. "Sorry," he said gruffly. "Guess I let my attention wander."

She bent to pick up a small, flat rock. "Steven and I spent hours skipping rocks when we were kids, seeing who could achieve the most skips or the farthest distance. Everything was a competition between us, and there were always prizes for the winners—I'd have to take his turn doing dishes or he'd have to take mine folding clothes."

"And did you honor those agreements?"

"Of course," she said with a lift of her chin. "We didn't welsh on bets."

Spotting a good skipping rock near his foot, Aaron scooped it up. "Bet I can skip farther than you."

She giggled. "Didn't you hear me say I spent my entire childhood practicing?"

"I've tossed a few rocks in my time, too."

Her skeptical snort made him laugh. "Bring it on, city boy."

He caught her wrist when she started to draw back for her throw. "Hang on. We haven't determined the prize yet."

"If you win I'll wash the dinner dishes?" she suggested.

He shook his head. "I clean as I go. There's little left to wash."

"Oh. Then whoever loses has to cook dinner tomorrow evening?"

She seemed to be making the assumption that he would still be there tomorrow evening, and she was probably right. He was in no hurry to leave, and he'd been assured the cabin was available through the weekend. Might as well take advantage of it. "I guess we could do that, but it's sort of a dull bet."

She planted her hands on her hips and looked at him in challenge. "Okay, fine, you come up with the prize."

"A date."

Her eyebrows rose. "A date?"

"Yeah. I win, you take me out for an evening you plan. If you win, I'll do the same for you."

She frowned. "If you win, I have to take you out on a date," she repeated. "Totally up to me what we do."

"Right. And I'll expect a good time. Within reason," he added with a reassuring smile. "Doesn't have to be fancy or expensive, but I'll expect to be entertained."

Her blue eyes sparkled with a hint of the competitive nature she'd nurtured in her youth. Her unpainted lips curved into an intrigued smile. "And if I win, you have to treat me to an evening of entertainment."

"Exactly."

"You're on, city boy. But I warn you, I'm going to

expect something more interesting than dinner and a movie. If it's a bet, you'd better bring your A-game when it comes to creativity."

"Same goes."

She cocked an eyebrow at him. "Something tells me this isn't the first time you've done this."

"Skipped a rock?" He tossed the flat pebble into the air and caught it deftly.

"No. Did the date challenge thing."

He thought of an interesting evening provided to him by a certain young woman who'd been confident she could beat him at Trivial Pursuit. She'd somehow scrounged up VIP seats for a Texas Rangers game, and dinner reservations at one of the hottest new restaurants in Dallas. Belinda had come from an oil dynasty, but he hadn't been overly impressed by the money she'd spent. He'd had a great time, they'd dated for another couple months before drifting apart, and they remained friends still.

"What makes you think that?" he asked Shelby blandly.

She studied him from beneath lowered brows, then turned toward the water again. "We'd better do this before it gets too dark to count skips."

Aaron flipped and caught his stone again. One way or another, he and Shelby would be spending another evening together. Frankly, he didn't care who achieved the greatest number of skips. As far as he was concerned, it was a win-win contest.

He won by one skip.

Shelby sighed gustily. "That boat wake took mine under."

"Two out of three?" he offered.

"No." She tossed her hair. "It was a fair bet. I'll just have to think of something creative to do with you."

He laughed and tugged at one of her curls. "There are just so many ways I could respond to that."

Her cheeks might have darkened, but she looked away before he could be sure. "Behave yourself."

"I guess I'd better," he replied with mock regret. "I'd hate to have your dad, grandfather, uncle and brother show up at my door to defend your honor."

"I beg your pardon?" She scooped up a sizable rock and juggled it from one hand to another. "I defend my own honor."

Still grinning, Aaron lifted both palms toward her in a conciliatory gesture. "Message received."

"Good." She lobbed the rock into the water with a noisy splash. "So, tomorrow afternoon we're going out on the water with Steven. How about Friday evening for our date? That will give me time to come up with something clever."

"That works for me."

She laughed softly. "You're something else, Aaron Walker."

He had no idea what that meant. The way she said it made it sound like a compliment, but with Shelby, there was no telling, really. He liked that about her.

Reaching out to her on impulse, he tugged her into his arms, his mouth hovering just above her smile. "I need to kiss you now," he said.

Obligingly, she wrapped her arms around his neck, looking up at him with wide eyes. "Is Landon watching?"

"I have no idea." Unable to resist a moment longer, he pressed his lips to hers.

The kiss warmed, deepened, lasted a long time.

Aaron didn't know if Terrence Landon or total strangers or Shelby's entire family could see them, nor did he care at that moment. He'd thought about kissing her all through dinner. He might as well admit it—he'd been wanting to taste her again since that brief kiss in her car yesterday. And it had nothing to do with any part he was playing, any plot she had concocted. He liked her, enjoyed her…wanted her. Wanted her so badly that he had to fight an urge to tumble her onto the beach and show her exactly how desirable he found her.

Reluctantly lifting his mouth from hers, he remembered the code word they'd teasingly chosen for a warning of danger ahead. "Minnesota," he murmured.

Looking a little dazed, she blinked. He didn't give her a chance to respond, but drew back and took her hand in his again to head back up the bank to his cabin.

He reminded himself that he had several days yet to enjoy Shelby's company. He was determined to do that without anyone getting hurt. She knew he was here only temporarily, and he knew there was nowhere else she wanted to be. It had even been her quirky idea to publicly send him away when it was time for him to go. There was no real peril to either of them—which didn't explain why he was suddenly, uncharacteristically edgy. Maybe it was the uncertainty of his own future. Or maybe just a natural reluctance to say goodbye to this charming new friend who didn't seem to think any less of him because of his situation.

He'd always tended to live in the present, enjoy the moment, seize the day. For the rest of this week, he'd stick with that practice. He'd worry about next week as the time drew nearer, he decided as Shelby looked up at him with a smile.

* * *

"It's getting pretty dark. I could drive you around to your place," Aaron offered a short while later, after they'd each had a lemon bar and he'd sampled one of her cookies.

Though she thought it was nice that he'd offered, Shelby shook her head with a smile. "That's not necessary, but thanks. I could ride home from here blindfolded, but our security lighting is good enough to get me there safely."

"I guess I forget this whole place is your front yard."

"Exactly." She threw a leg over her bike and kicked the stand out of the way. "I'll see you tomorrow, Aaron. Thanks for the dinner."

"Thank you for sharing it with me," he returned. "I enjoyed the company."

So polite, she mused as she turned her bike and began to pedal. Hard to believe the impeccably well-mannered gentleman who'd just seen her off had rocked her world with a steamy stolen kiss less than an hour earlier. She still got shivery inside when she remembered that kiss. She expected that reaction would last a while.

Passing the private drive sign, she bit her lip as she pedaled past her parents' house. She was thinking about the word Aaron had murmured after he'd kissed her senseless. Minnesota, the joking code she'd given him for danger. Had he implied that their embrace had been dangerous for her—or for him? The latter seemed unlikely. Obviously, he'd been teasing. He did that a lot—which was yet another difference between him and Andrew, or at least the Andrew who'd spent almost two weeks here in the course of his job.

She had to chuckle when she remembered that rock-skipping contest. She blamed her loss on the effort she'd

had to make to hide her foolish reactions to Aaron's
smiles, his touch. Just by holding her hand, he'd made
her pulse race in a way that she'd hoped she concealed
from him, though she'd been all too aware of it, herself. He'd winked at her just as she'd turned to release
her stone, and while it probably hadn't been intended
as sabotage, that engaging wink had still scrambled her
circuits. That was her story, and she was sticking to it,
though she would keep the excuse to herself.

So now she owed him a date. And she was the one
who'd loftily proclaimed that a dinner-and-movie outing
wasn't creative or adventurous enough. What was she
going to do to entertain Aaron for an evening?

Her front tire wobbled a little when a few intrigu-
ing possibilities popped unbidden into her mind. She'd
have to put a stop to that train of thought quickly or risk
crashing her bike before she arrived at her door. Once
she was safely inside—well, then she'd be free to fan-
tasize all she wanted about sexy Aaron Walker.

Chapter Six

Even on vacations, Aaron didn't tend to be a late sleeper. He was up with the sun the next morning, opening the blinds to let in the light. The brief rainfall during the night had been just enough to leave everything clean and fresh this morning, almost begging him to go outside and appreciate.

There was no movement from the cabin next door, and the blinds there were still tightly closed, he noted before heading for the shower. He wondered if Andrew had dug up anything interesting on Terrence Landon, because Aaron had noted nothing particularly remarkable.

After a quick shower and shave, he dressed in a worn gray T-shirt from a Springsteen concert seven summers earlier and a pair of charcoal shorts made of a quick-dry fabric for water sports. He zipped his wallet into a waterproof bag and shoved it in his back pocket, then buttoned his cell phone, which was already protected by a waterproof case, into the cargo pocket on his right thigh. Water sandals, sunglasses and his Rangers ball cap completed his ultracasual outfit.

Man, he thought, he could get used to dressing like this every day. No tie, no jacket, no socks, for that matter. Maybe his next job should be outdoors. He didn't mind hard work, but he wouldn't care if he never wore another necktie.

He ate a bagel with chocolate-hazelnut spread for breakfast, then took out his phone and dialed his brother. "Have you found anything on Landon?" he asked as soon as he heard Andrew's voice.

"I take it you're still at the resort?"

"Yeah. Thought I'd hang around through the weekend while I do some internet searches for my next career plans. It's a nice place. Nice people."

"They are," Andrew agreed.

Aaron thought of the brochure he'd found on the floor. "But you weren't planning to come back here, were you?"

"Not anytime soon," Andrew replied after a very brief hesitation. "I didn't see any need to do so once the job ended."

Aaron thought the Bell family would be disappointed if they heard that. They seemed to think Andrew had become a friend while he'd worked for them, whereas he kept referring to them as clients. Aaron knew his twin well enough to figure out that something else was going on here, but also well enough to know that Andrew would tell him what it was in his own good time. Prodding would get him nowhere.

He changed the subject. "So about Terrence Landon..."

"The license number you gave me belongs to a rental.

It was leased in a woman's name, Marie Jonas. Haven't yet found anything to tell me who she is."

"I haven't seen a woman around. A man visited yesterday. I've got another license plate for you."

"Did you notice anything suspicious about the guy's visit?"

"Other than that both of them looked nervous and distrustful of me, not really. But to be honest, Landon could be jumpy because Shelby's been spying on him, probably not quite as subtly as she thinks."

Andrew gave a short bark of laughter. "You'd better tell her to back off before she gets charged with stalking."

"Already have. She has reason to be suspicious, the guy seems downright weird. But other than peeking at me through his blinds, I haven't seen him do anything over the top. Did you find anything on him?"

"Not so far. No record I can find of a Terrence Landon in marketing in Austin. Doesn't mean he's a fake, just that I haven't found him yet."

Which raised Aaron's suspicions even further. Was the guy really here under an assumed name? And if so, why?

"Everything you've told me raises flags," Andrew continued. "The name, the rental car, paying in cash, the stream of visitors, staying inside at a place most people go to for outdoor sports. But has it occurred to you his visitors could be there for sex? This could all be nothing more than a cheating spouse or partner trying to stay low."

"It occurred to me. Not ruling it out, though I didn't get that vibe from them yesterday."

"I'll run this new number, see what else I can find on Landon. Can't get to it immediately, I've got a security consultation in Plano this morning. Having lunch with the CEO and a few bigwigs, doing a factory walk-through afterward."

"Can't see that there's any rush. If Landon checks out before we find anything, I don't think anyone will be sad to see him go. Whatever he's up to, Shelby doesn't want him using her family's resort for it, but he hasn't shown any hurry to leave yet."

"Then I'll look into it when I can."

"Thanks, Andrew."

"You seem awfully eager to set Shelby's mind at ease."

Was Andrew sensing something in his voice when he spoke of Shelby? It wasn't easy to slip anything past his twin. "I told you yesterday that I like her. I like them all. Spent some time with Steven yesterday. Nice guy."

"Yeah. Restless."

"Did he mention that to you?"

"No. Just picked up on it while I was there."

No surprise there, either. Aaron cleared his throat, wondering what else his brother was picking up on. "I'd better let you get ready for your meetings. Give me a call if you come up with anything interesting."

"Tell everyone there I said hello."

"I will."

Disconnecting the call, Aaron frowned down at the phone for a few minutes. There was something in his brother's voice when they talked about the Bell family… something Aaron wished he understood better. As soon as he got back to Dallas, he was going to do a little pry-ing of his own.

With nothing pressing to do before meeting Shelby and Steven, he let himself out of his cabin. He noticed that Terrence Landon stood on the porch next door, glancing at his watch as if waiting for a late arrival.

"Good morning," Aaron called out after locking his door, settling his cap more snugly on his head. "Looks like it's going to be another nice day."

Landon scowled at him, nodded curtly and backed into his cabin, closing the door sharply. Shaking his head, Aaron started walking toward the marina, exchanging greetings with a more sociable senior citizen couple he passed along the way. A green golf cart carrying two members of the resort housekeeping staff buzzed past and he waved at them, too. He was sure he could find something entertaining to do for a couple of hours. Though his first choice would have been to spend time with Shelby, he could bide his time until she joined him later.

It was far from the first time that Shelby worked all morning with a swimsuit beneath her top and shorts. That was one of the best parts about her bookkeeping job, working her own hours in the private office with little formal contact with the resort guests. She had quite a bit to do before meeting Aaron and Steven for water sports, so she was at the computer early, her fingers flying over the keyboard, numbers and forms flashing across the monitor screen. She sipped coffee at her desk, not even taking a break until she'd completed her day's tasks. Only then did she stretch and look at the clock. It was straight-up noon. No wonder her tummy was starting to growl. Breakfast had been hours ago.

After straightening her desk, she headed downstairs. Sometimes she ate lunch at her place, or with various family members at one of the houses, but she had no plans today. Might as well eat in the grill, she figured.

The grill was busy, almost all the tables and most of the bar stools occupied. Most of the diners were guests from the campgrounds and motel, but one table was surrounded by the male members of her family. Her dad, uncle, grandfather and brother were all there—and they'd been joined by Aaron, she noted with a flutter of pleasure at seeing him. As if he'd sensed her presence, he looked around, smiled and motioned for her to join them.

Seeing her approaching, her father snagged an empty chair and maneuvered it into a space opened when the others moved closer to each other. Shelby helped herself to a diet soda from the fountain behind the counter, then scooted sideways into the chair. It was a tight fit, but she managed to squeeze in between Aaron and her dad. "Am I interrupting anything?" she asked cheerily.

"Would it make any difference if you were?"

She wrinkled her nose in response to her brother's dry response. "No. But carry on."

It looked as though the men hadn't been there long. They'd barely started on their burgers. Aaron, she noted, was having grilled chicken again. He really was a healthy eater. She'd have to keep that in mind while planning the date she owed him.

"Want a sandwich, Shelby?" her mother called out from behind the counter.

"Got time to put another chicken breast on the grill?"

"Of course." Her mother opened the fridge.

"We were just outlining the work that has to be done around here during the next few months," Bryan informed her while she waited for her lunch.

"Like the marina remodel?"

"That. A lot of painting and weatherproofing. Need to put a new roof on Cabin Two next week, and on the motel before winter. Still thinking about putting in two new RV pads over by the boat storage to use for holiday overflow. The usual maintenance and grounds upkeep."

Shelby happened to be looking at her brother while her uncle listed only some of the jobs scheduled for the upcoming months. Steven's jaw seemed to tighten a little more with each task mentioned.

"How much of the work will you hire out?" Aaron asked, seemingly fascinated by the inner workings of the resort.

"As little as possible," Bryan answered with a shrug. "Like everyone else these days, we try to keep our expenses down. The whole family will chip in when not taking care of their other chores, along with some of the seasonal workers we employ during summer break from school."

"I wield a mean paintbrush," Shelby said.

"But don't let her near a nail gun," Steven said with a grimace.

"That was just one time!" she protested indignantly.

"And I could have lost an eye."

She snorted. "I missed you by a good three or four inches."

Steven looked significantly at Aaron. "Like I said."

"So, anyway," Bryan said to Shelby's dad, as if continuing a conversation that had started before she'd joined them, "I'm going to hire Bubba and those two friends of his for the summer. We know Bubba's a good worker and he vouches for his friends. Tomorrow's their last day of school this semester."

C.J. nodded. "Bubba's a good kid. Not the brightest bulb in the box, but he gives it his all. I say go for it."

"Is that the boy who wore his pants down around his butt last summer?" Pop demanded with a scowl.

"Well, he did until you threatened to make him wear striped suspenders," Steven said with a chuckle. "After that, he bought a good belt."

"He'll work hard for us, Dad," Bryan assured him. "And I'll tell them all to keep their shorts covered."

Aaron sipped his lemonade, sitting back and listening to the conversation. Shelby wondered how many business-related meals took place around his own family's lunch table. She would bet there'd been more than a few.

"Steven, I need you to set the new charcoal grill in Site Thirty after lunch," Bryan mumbled around a mouthful of burger. "Going to be busy this weekend, and we'll need it."

"Some yahoo backed his trailer into the old grill and broke it right in half," Pop grumbled to Aaron. "Nowhere near the RV pad. Don't know what he was thinking."

Steven glanced at his watch. "I told Aaron we'd take out a couple of Jet Skis this afternoon."

"I'll help you install the grill, and we can play afterward," Aaron suggested.

"I'll help, too," Shelby offered. "I was planning to join you in the water, anyway. I've finished just about everything I have to do in the office today."

"But no nail gun for you," Aaron told her, grinning.

She rolled her eyes. "I'm aware that we won't need a nail gun to set a grill in concrete."

"Just saying. I'd kind of like to keep my eyes."

Bryan gave them a crooked smile. "I'm not sure about letting you three loose on a job, but I've got too much else to do myself, so I guess I'll have to trust you with it. Unless there's something you'd rather do, Aaron. After all, you already helped me unload that trailer at the storage building. Then you spent a couple hours helping C.J. in the marina. Don't feel like you have to help Steven with the grill. He's perfectly capable of putting it in himself."

"I was looking for something to do when I saw you unloading the trailer," Aaron said with a slight shrug. "And I was interested in what goes into running the marina. I learned a lot I never really thought about before. I don't mind helping with the grill, either."

Steven nodded. "I'd appreciate it. Besides, the faster we're done, the sooner we can get out on the water."

Shelby glanced up with a smile when her mother set a plate in front of her. "Thanks, Mom."

Pop was looking hard at Aaron. "You remember that guy who worked the gate for us last year? The older man with the prosthetic leg? He passed away a couple months ago. Got an infection he couldn't shake."

"I'm sorry to hear that, but I didn't know him," Aaron replied patiently while everyone else shook their heads. "I've never been here before this week."

"Oh, that's right. That was your, er, identical twin brother." Pop winked.

While the others either groaned or chuckled, Shelby studied her grandfather closely. Did he really believe Aaron was Andrew, or was he putting them on? It was hard to tell with Pop. Always had been.

Her dad began a familiar diatribe about the outrageous cost of marine fuel, which led to an oft-repeated discussion of the rising prices of liability insurance and other expenses of business. Shelby ate her sandwich while the men complained. Aaron commented a few times, but mostly seemed content to listen. He fit in well here, she mused, just as his brother had.

She wondered if Andrew would be back to see them

OFFICIAL OPINION POLL

Dear Reader,

Since you are a book enthusiast, we would like to know what you think.

Inside you will find a short Opinion Poll. Please participate in our poll by sharing your opinion on 3 subjects that are very important to all of us.

To thank you for your participation, we would like to send you **2 FREE BOOKS** and **2 FREE GIFTS!**

Please enjoy them with our compliments.

Sincerely,

Pam Powers

YOUR OPINION POLL
THANK-YOU FREE GIFTS INCLUDE:

▶ **2 HARLEQUIN® SPECIAL EDITION BOOKS**

▶ **2 LOVELY SURPRISE GIFTS**

OFFICIAL OPINION POLL

YOUR OPINION COUNTS!
Please check TRUE or FALSE below to express your opinion about the following statements:

Q1 Do you believe in "true love"?

"TRUE LOVE HAPPENS ONLY ONCE IN A LIFETIME."
○ TRUE
○ FALSE

Q2 Do you think marriage has any value in today's world?

"YOU CAN BE TOTALLY COMMITTED TO SOMEONE WITHOUT BEING MARRIED."
○ TRUE
○ FALSE

Q3 What kind of books do you enjoy?

"A GREAT NOVEL MUST HAVE A HAPPY ENDING."
○ TRUE
○ FALSE

YES! I have placed my sticker in the space provided below. Please send me the **2 FREE books** and **2 FREE gifts** for which I qualify. I understand that I am under no obligation to purchase anything further, as explained on the back of this card.

235/335 HDL FVN6

FIRST NAME · LAST NAME

ADDRESS

APT.# · CITY

STATE/PROV. · ZIP/POSTAL CODE

Printed in the U.S.A.
© 2012 HARLEQUIN ENTERPRISES LIMITED.

anytime soon. Apparently, he'd recommended the resort to Aaron. It would have been nice if both of them could have come, though even if they had, she thought she would still have been drawn this strongly to Aaron.

Steven gathered his disposable plate, napkin and drink cup. "I'll load up the grill and supplies."

Wiping his mouth, Aaron rose. "I'm ready."

"I'll finish my lunch and join you at the site," Shelby told them.

She watched them walk out, though she found her attention focusing on Aaron. He looked darned good in his T-shirt and shorts, she thought with a very faint sigh. Those long, tanned legs were sexy as all get-out, and the way his shorts skimmed his lean hips drew her gaze straight to his nice, firm butt. She didn't usually notice guys' backsides all that much, but there was nothing about Aaron she didn't admire.

When he'd walked outside, she turned her attention back to her lunch. Her gaze collided with her dad's, and she realized that he'd been watching her watching Aaron. She cleared her throat and took a big bite of her sandwich, looking down at her plate to avoid her father's eyes as she chewed.

With three of them to do the job, it took less than an hour to set the new grill in concrete. Steven and Aaron dug the new hole with a post-hole digger and added a thin layer of gravel. Shelby helped Aaron steady the grill while Steven poured in the concrete mix, and then Shelby used a level to make sure the cooking surface was properly aligned. Leaving the concrete to set, they stashed their tools in the back of the utility ATV.

Steven dusted off his hands. "That didn't take long."

"Compared to the list your uncle recited at lunch, I'd

say this was one of the easier jobs on the near horizon,"
Aaron commented.

Steven nodded. "Yeah. We don't lack for projects to
tackle around here."

Most of which would be manual labor, Shelby
thought, though of course Steven would be in a super-
visory position even as he worked alongside the summer
workers. As the older generations retired, she and Steven and their cousins would take on even more management responsibilities—Lori, too, if she wanted, though
that seemed increasingly unlikely. With his degree in
business management and years of experience in the
business, Steven was fully qualified to run the place
eventually—as she was herself, for that matter.

Maggie had said many times that she never wanted
to be responsible for major business decisions, having no interest in numbers and legal regulations and
licenses and contract negotiations. She liked the per-
sonnel part—interviewing, hiring, supervising, firing
if necessary, though that was hardly her favorite chore.
She had double majored in human resources and Span-
ish, and was already happily settled into her niche here.

With a degree in marketing and advertising, Hannah was a people person. She loved working the front
desk, greeting longtime guests, designing advertising
materials and especially the social media part of her
promotional duties. Steven and Shelby were the ones
interested in upper management—actually running the
business itself, which their father and uncle had been
doing together since Pop had stepped down from full-
time administration a few years ago. At least Shelby
was interested in that future. Honestly, she couldn't say
what Steven wanted these days.

Whatever his thoughts about the future, Steven

seemed to enjoy playing with them that afternoon. They sped out of the marina on resort-owned personal watercraft. Proving he'd had plenty of experience with the machines, Aaron raced across the glittering surface of the lake with the same ease as Shelby and Steven. They laughed, explored nooks and inlets, jumped boat wakes, kicked up joyous tails of water behind them. Aaron was flirty with Shelby—though she couldn't have said whether it was because of her cover story or simply because he liked flirting—and jovial with Steven. Both of them enjoyed his company.

Perhaps Shelby had to make an occasional effort to focus on her driving rather than admiring how good Aaron looked straddling the powerful machine, his dark hair whipping in the wind, his white teeth gleaming with his grins. He gave her a few appreciative looks, too, which did wonders for her ego. Her swimsuit was a purple two-piece cut more for function than fashion, but she still thought it flattered her. It highlighted her toned arms, legs and midriff without causing her to worry about anything showing that shouldn't.

They stopped the machines in a quiet cove, took off their life vests and dove into the water for a swim, leaving wallets, cell phones and sunglasses in the watercraft storage compartments. The men had shed their T-shirts, draping them over the handlebars of their skis. All three of them were competitive, and soon they were racing. Steven and Aaron were evenly matched, and Shelby held her own despite her smaller stature.

She couldn't remember the last time she'd laughed quite so much.

"Oh, man," Aaron said, finally slowing down to paddle lazily on his back. "This is the life."

Steven climbed back onto his watercraft, pushing a hand through his wet hair. "It's a good life," he agreed.

"It's a great life," Shelby said, treading water beside her machine. "We work hard, we play hard, we're surrounded by nature and people we love. What's not to like?"

She watched as Aaron and Steven shared a slightly rueful glance. "Maybe that *surrounded* part," Aaron murmured.

Steven grunted. "You got that right."

"Oh, come on, you guys. You know you love your families."

"We do." Still floating, Aaron smiled at her. "Doesn't mean we want them watching and commenting on everything we do."

Steven nodded as he donned his life vest and snapped the fastenings. "Amen."

Shelby sighed and shook a wet curl out of her face. Aaron seemed completely sympathetic to her brother's growing wanderlust. Now that she knew how he felt about working with his own family, she supposed it made sense that he'd understand how Steven felt.

Steven had taken his watch out of the watercraft's storage compartment. Glancing at it, he said, "I'd better get back. It's after four, and I still have some mowing to do. No need for you two to rush back, though. Take your time. Have fun."

"See you later, Steven."

Steven nodded to Aaron, then gave Shelby a little wave. "Be careful."

He leaned the watercraft into a turn and gunned the engine, speeding out into the open lake and toward home. Shelby was left wondering just what he'd meant by that final warning. Was it the obvious interpretation—that she should be careful in the water, with the Jet Ski? Or a more subtle caution that she should be careful about her probably obvious attraction to Aaron?

Or was she just overthinking everything today?

Exasperated with herself, she swam to her machine, preparing to hoist herself onto it. Before she could do so, she was pulled completely underwater. She emerged laughing and sputtering, slapping a handful of water directly into Aaron's face. He grinned and tossed his head, slinging droplets from the ends of his dark hair, some of which landed on her cheeks.

"Sorry," he said. "Couldn't resist."

"You couldn't resist dunking me?"

His smile faded a little. His dark eyes locked with hers. "I couldn't resist putting my hands on you."

"Oh." Had the water suddenly gotten hotter? She felt a definite wave of heat course through her and was almost surprised that steam didn't rise from her skin. "Um—"

"No one's watching," he murmured, reaching out to draw her closer with his left arm around her waist. He braced his other arm on her watercraft to support them. "I'm not playing a part. So if you want me to back off, just give me a shove."

She put a hand on his shoulder, but only to steady herself in the water. She had no intention of pushing him away. His skin was slick and wet beneath her palm. Her fingers flexed instinctively into the muscle beneath. "I have to kiss you now," she said gravely, trying not to smile.

He grinned at her deliberate quote of him from last night. "Then I guess I have to let you."

Because he was leaving it to her, she floated closer to him, wrapping her right arm around his neck and resting her other hand on the watercraft for balance. Their legs tangled beneath the water, his rough, hers smooth. Her bare tummy pressed against his. The thin fabric of her top was the only barrier between her breasts and his broad, only lightly furred chest, but even that suddenly felt intrusive.

She tilted her head a little and took a tasting nip at his mouth, licking lake water from his lower lip. It was a freshwater lake, so the slightly salty taste must be from him. She liked it. Her hand slipped into the wet hair at the back of his head as she kissed him more thoroughly. And now he was an active participant, his lips claiming hers, his tongue plunging into the depths of her mouth to tease and explore.

The embrace escalated rapidly from light and teasing to sizzling, hungry. Here was the passion that had been missing with Pete, she thought dazedly. The urgency. The bone-deep craving. She felt the hard ridge of his arousal against her abdomen and wondered if it was possible that Aaron could want her as badly. And if so, was it only because she was available? Or because he really did like her?

Be careful, her brother had warned. She would do well to listen to him for once. But she had never been the type to simply do what she was told, especially by her siblings.

Leaving only an inch between their mouths, Aaron gazed into her eyes and she wondered if her expression looked as dazzled as she felt. "I think the water's starting to boil," he murmured.

"I wouldn't be surprised." Brushing her lips against his one more time, she drew her arm from around his neck and swam backward a stroke, putting a little distance between them. "We should get these back to the marina."

She was pleased by the reluctance in his nod. "I know."

Though she didn't need the assistance, he still gave her a boost onto her seat, letting his hand linger just a bit longer than necessary on her bare thigh. She wasn't at all cool, but she shivered a little in response to the touch. After a moment, Aaron swam away, bracing his arms on his watercraft to give himself a boost upward. Water sluiced off his sleek back, and Shelby gave a little sigh she hoped he didn't hear.

With the powerful machine between his legs, he glanced over his shoulder, grinned, then started his engine. "See you at the marina."

He was skimming out of the cove before she could even respond.

Having put away the watercraft and chatted for a few minutes with C.J., Aaron and Shelby went into the store through the marina entrance. Swimming always made Aaron hungry, and he told Shelby he was in the mood for something unhealthy and indulgent, which seemed to amuse her. Actually, he was in the mood for another couple of hours alone with Shelby—preferably somewhere with a bed—but he told himself he'd have to make do with sugar.

They ended up back in the grill, which was quickly becoming one of Aaron's favorite places.

"Looks like the two of you had a good time today," Sarah commented, smiling at them from behind the counter.

Aaron chuckled. He and Shelby weren't the only ones in the place wearing damp bathing suits beneath other clothes and glowing pink from sun and exercise, their hair mussed from wind-drying. "I had a great time. Your kids are just a bit competitive, aren't they?"

Sarah groaned good-humoredly. "You can say that again. From the time Steven and Shelby could talk, they were challenging each other to various competitions and making bets on the outcome. Sometimes we had to step in, like when Steven once had to agree to do Shelby's homework for a week, or when Shelby lost a bet that would have her writing her brother's final essay for junior English class, but usually we just let them work it out for themselves."

Aaron thought it best not to mention the bet he and Shelby had made last night. When he and Shelby went out for whatever activities she planned tomorrow, he'd leave it up to her to make any explanations to her family.

Motioning them onto stools at the counter, Sarah said, "I bet you'd like a snack. Water sports always work up an appetite."

"You read my mind," he told her.

"What can I get you? Pie? Ice cream?"

Knowing he would have to argue with her—as always—to take his money afterward, Aaron requested a slice of lemon meringue pie and an iced tea. Tart, cold pie sounded delicious after being out in the sun.

"Shelby?" her mother asked.

"I think I'll have a root beer float," Shelby decided. "But I'll get it, Mom."

"Don't be silly. Talk with your friend. I'm back here, anyway."

She served them efficiently, cut a slice of apple pie and another slice of lemon pie for another couple who'd wandered in, then leaned on the counter to chat with Aaron and Shelby.

"C.J.'s had some short ribs in the smoker all day today," she told Aaron. "We'd love to have you join us for dinner later, if you like."

"I do love ribs," he admitted. "I'd be pleased to join you, if it wouldn't be an imposition."

Sarah laughed softly, looking very much like Shelby when she did so. "You've spent half your time with us helping Steven and Bryan—and probably Shelby," she added with a meaningful look at her daughter. "Feeding you a few ribs is the least we can do. Besides, we'd enjoy having you. Everyone's going to be there except Maggie. She had plans with friends this evening, and she's already left. We'll eat after C.J. closes the marina at seven."

"This pie should've just about worn off by then," he said, making a show of checking his watch. He had time to shower and make some calls before dinner.

C.J. rushed into the grill then. Aaron felt his stomach tighten after one look at the older man's face. Sarah set down her pie server. "What's wrong?"

C.J.'s voice was grim. "Steven's hurt. An ambulance is on its way. We need to go."

Both Aaron and Shelby were on their feet now.

"What happened?" Shelby asked, one hand at her throat.

"He flipped the mower over on himself. I don't know how bad it is. Bryan just called and said come. They're at Site Thirty-eight."

Sarah gasped and rushed around the counter just as Linda entered, the look on her face making it obvious she knew what had happened. "Go," she said to Sarah. "I'll work the grill until I hear from you. If anyone needs anything from the store, I'll just run back and forth."

Aaron shook his head. "I can run the store and the marina. I've worked a cash register before. The rest of you go. Take care of Steven."

They didn't even linger to argue with him. He saw Lori rush through the entryway just in time to join the rest of her family as they ran from the building.

Aaron turned to Linda then. "How bad is it?"

"I don't know," she murmured, her eyes haunted. "Bryan said he was unconscious when they found him. Bryan's gone to tell Mimi and Pop, then he'll head over here to help out until we know something."

They looked at each other when they heard a siren pass outside the building. "I'm sure he'll be fine," Aaron said, wanting to reassure himself as well as Steven's aunt. He liked Steven. He didn't even want to consider the possibility of a bad outcome.

Glancing across the entryway, he saw two middle-aged women going into the store just as a young couple with a toddler entered the diner. "I'll handle the store," he said to Linda. "I'll let you know if I need any help."

She nodded, pushed a strand of graying brown hair from her face and pasted a taut, fake smile on her face before turning to wait on the newcomers.

Chapter Seven

It was just after seven-thirty that evening when Shelby stood in the doorway of the store, her arrival not yet noticed. She watched as Aaron chatted easily with a middle-aged couple she recognized as first-time visitors to the resort who'd checked in a few days earlier. A few canned goods and bottled waters sat on the counter beside the register, and he rang up two candy bars while Shelby watched. The store should have closed half an hour ago, along with the grill and marina, but her aunt and uncle had made the call to leave them open a little longer this evening. Shelby suspected it was because both of them had been too anxious to wait patiently for word about Steven's condition, preferring to stay busy instead. Obviously Aaron had agreed.

From the snatches of conversation she overheard, the couple was telling him about their morning at a nearby golf course, boasting about their scores. She didn't know if Aaron played golf or had any interest what-ever in the sport, but he listened politely and congrat-ulated them with obvious sincerity on their morning's achievements. They left with their purchases stashed in reusable canvas bags, smiling and greeting Shelby as they passed her on their way out.

Spotting her then, Aaron moved toward her, search-ing her face. "Your aunt told me Steven's going to be okay?" he asked, the question at the end seeking con-firmation.

She nodded wearily. "He has a concussion and a bro-ken bone in his leg, some nasty bruises and a couple of cracked ribs. They're keeping him overnight for ob-servation, but he should be fine. It was a clean break, so he didn't need surgery for his leg, and it should heal without any complications, but he'll have to stay off it for a few weeks. He's going to hate that."

Aaron let out a deep exhale of relief. "I'm glad to hear he wasn't seriously injured. I know you were all terrified for him. I was, myself."

She rested a hand on his arm. "Thank you for help-ing out here."

"Your uncle took over the marina after Steven was transported to the hospital. I just ran the cash register in here," he said self-deprecatingly. "I wasn't very busy, though I think your aunt has been kept hopping in the diner. You weren't even gone very long."

"Mom and Dad sent everyone away as soon as we knew Steven was out of danger. I'm going to close the store while Aunt Linda wraps up in the grill. Lori and Mimi are at Mom and Dad's, getting dinner ready. Dad will join us for dinner, but Mom insisted on spending the night at the hospital with Steven. There's a pullout bed in his room for family."

"Does she need anything for the night? I'd be happy to take her a bag while the rest of you have dinner and rest."

She shook her head, touched that he was offering even more assistance. "She said she has everything she needs for tonight. She's going to sleep in her clothes and she can get a toothbrush there. Have dinner with us, instead. We'll be eating late, around eight-thirty, so I'm going to rush home and shower first. I'm still wearing my swimsuit under my clothes."

He nodded. "I'll do the same. What can I do to help you close up in here first?"

An hour later, they sat with the rest of the family over plates of ribs, potato salad and corn on the cob. Though the food was enjoyed, the overall mood was a bit somber, despite the general relief that Steven would fully recover. They'd all had a major scare and it would take a while for that shock to pass. Looking around the big table that held all her family except for her mother, brother and two cousins, Shelby acknowledged silently that she was far from ready to let go of any of them.

"He's going to be off work for at least a month," her dad said to Bryan, looking grim.

Bryan nodded. "We can get by with the summer help, put off a few projects until he's up and around again. Only thing I'm concerned about is that roofing project on Cabin Two. Need to get that done before the next big rain. We were lucky the rain last night was a light one. The materials are supposed to be in tomorrow, and we were going to start on it Saturday, try to finish it up this weekend. Don't think I can do it by myself. We might just have to hire out that job so we can get it out of the way as soon as possible."

"Let me help," Aaron offered, to no one's surprise

by now, Shelby thought. "I've got nothing pressing to get to for a few days yet. I worked construction a couple of summers in college, so I know how to lay shingles. I always liked working with my hands."

It was also no surprise to Shelby that it took him less than ten minutes of arguing to convince them. Even to almost make them think they were doing him a favor to let him help.

"Have you ever considered politics as your next potential career pursuit?" she asked him with a laugh when she drove him to his cabin in a golf cart after dinner. They both knew he could easily have walked back, but they'd taken advantage of the excuse to spend a little more time alone.

"I have no interest at all in politics," he assured her. "Why?"

She parked the cart in his drive and smiled at him. "You are one smooth talker. By the time we left, you were practically thanking everyone for letting you help around this place. And they were buying it!"

"They did say they would refuse to accept a dime from me for my stay here," he pointed out. "I've been fishing and swimming and been fed ribs—I'm having a great vacation, and I even enjoy working with your family. I'd say I'm getting the better part of the deal."

Definitely a slick talker, she thought, stifling a smile. "You might not think so when you're up on that roof at high noon Saturday."

He shrugged. "I spent one whole summer doing construction work in a year that set heat records, with temperatures over a hundred nearly every afternoon. And I still liked the work just fine. A weekend roofing project will be a piece of cake after that."

"I know Uncle Bryan really appreciates your offer

to help," she said more seriously. "He didn't seem too worried about putting off the other big projects until Steven's back on his feet, but they've had this roofing job scheduled for weeks."

"I'm just glad your brother will be okay." He climbed out of the cart. "Would you like to come in? I bought some herbal tea in town yesterday. My mom's an herbal-tea junkie, and I've gotten in the habit of drinking it in the evenings."

She paused only a moment, deliberating the wisdom of going inside with him, then slid out of the cart, almost defiantly stuffing the key into her pocket. "I like a cup of tea in the evenings myself."

Aaron was already digging in his pocket for his own keys, but he suddenly hesitated. "This won't cause problems for you with your family, will it? Coming inside with me at night, I mean."

She laughed in disbelief. "Aaron, I'm twenty-five years old. I don't have a curfew, nor do I answer to my parents about where I spend my evenings."

He chuckled in response to her defensive tone. "Okay, just checking."

"Besides," she muttered, following him inside, "Lori still lives at home and who knows where she's been spending her weekends lately. She says she's hanging out with college friends, but I'm not sure."

His face averted from her, Aaron tossed his keys on the bar. "You think she has a secret boyfriend?"

"I think she's hanging with a questionable crowd," she admitted. "She doesn't introduce us to her friends and she's been acting…well, differently lately. Part of it I think is just the natural process of separating herself from family, growing up, establishing her own identity. But I still worry."

Filling the teakettle, he spoke over the running water. "Could be if you confronted her she'd say pretty much what you just told me. She's over eighteen, too old for a curfew and doesn't need family approval for her friends."

Shelby made a face. "You're absolutely right, of course. I was being hypocritical, wasn't I?"

"You were being concerned about your sister," he corrected, taking a box of tea from a cupboard.

They carried their cups to the couch, settling side by side on the cushions. Shelby set her cup on the low table in front of them with a long sigh. "What a day."

Setting his steaming cup next to hers, he turned toward her, his expression sympathetic. "It has been a long one, hasn't it?"

Thinking of all that had happened since her alarm had gone off that morning, she murmured, "You could say that again."

"I had a good time until your brother was hurt."

Massaging the back of her neck, she gave him a tired smile. "I'm glad. So did I."

"Turn around."

"What?"

"Your neck is bothering you. Let me massage it for you. I've been told I'm pretty good at it."

She would just bet he was. "I tensed up while we were waiting to hear about Steven."

He was already scooting her around. "You overdid it today."

"Not really. Just got a little overwhelmed."

"Understandable."

"I was so scared when I heard that Steven was hurt. Seeing him being driven away in that ambulance…" She shuddered.

"He'll be fine, Shelby. I was thrown from a horse at my uncle Jared's ranch when I was a teenager. Concussion, broken arm, a few cracked ribs—similar to your brother's injuries. I healed without any repercussions. The arm's as strong as ever, and if there was any permanent brain damage, no one would be able to tell the difference, anyway," he finished with a laugh.

"Funny." But his reassurances did make her feel better.

He tipped her head forward. She'd tied her damp hair into a loose braid after a fast shower before dinner. His thumbs pressed against her neck beneath the braid, rotated slowly. A moan of pleasure escaped her. "Feels good."

He slid his hands down to the junction of her neck and shoulder, and squeezed, working the tense knots he found there. "With everything that went on today, I didn't have much time to spy on my neighbor."

Her head down, her eyes closed, she felt her muscles stretch, go slack beneath his skilled hands. "You are very good at this," she murmured. "And to tell you the truth, I'd forgotten all about your neighbor."

His breath was warm on her skin when he spoke, his head bent close to her. "You mean you didn't come in to peek out my kitchen window?"

She laughed softly. "No, that wasn't why I came in."

She felt his lips brush the back of her neck and she shivered in response, her smile fading. "Nice to know," he said.

Drawing a long, deep breath, she turned on the couch to face him, resting one hand on his chest as she looked at him. His lips were curved into a faint smile, but his eyes had darkened with an intensity that reflected her own mounting desire. So much had happened in the past couple of days that her emotions were right under the surface. And she'd never been able to hide her feelings well. Aaron had to see how attracted she was to him.

She couldn't read him nearly as easily as he probably could her. Yet she saw the reciprocal awareness in his expression when he slowly lowered his mouth to hers. His lips moved hungrily against hers, his tongue teasing her lips apart to allow him access. She never even considered resisting. Burying her fingers in his hair, she crowded closer, craving more contact.

His right hand swept her back, tracing her through the thin mint-green top she'd donned after her quick shower. His left hand rested on her bare thigh, just below the hem of her khaki shorts. Heat radiated from his palm, spreading from her thigh upward to the now-tingling core of her. She pictured his hand moving upward, inward, and her stomach clenched. His other hand was already beneath her shirt, gliding against her back, sliding around her waist to rest thrillingly close to her breast.

The kiss grew more urgent, deepened until their mouths were fused, their tongues intimately tangled. Aaron's toned muscles were rigid beneath her seeking hands, and she could only imagine how hard the rest of him must be. She found out for certain when he leaned back and drew her with him so that she was lying mostly on top of him.

He wanted her. That knowledge was so heady, so overwhelming, that she trembled with it. She'd never burned quite like this, never wanted anyone quite so desperately. It was almost as terrifying as it was exhilarating. Too much, too soon, too risky. It had stung when Pete had bruised her pride; it would be so much worse if she let Aaron break her heart.

Swallowing hard, she peeled her lips from his and planted her hands on his chest, pushing herself a couple inches away from him. "I have to—" *think,* she almost said "—breathe," she substituted.

A long curl had escaped her braid, dangling into her face. Aaron reached up to tuck it gently behind her ear. "Oxygen is overrated."

She laughed unsteadily. "Still."

He kept his eyes on her face when he said in a low voice, "You know, I'd bet you could see the cabin next door very well from the window in the bedroom."

She shook her head at him, both amused and somewhat shaken by the suggestion. He wasn't pressuring her—but the significance behind his teasing comment had been clear enough. "The only two windows upstairs are at the front and back of the loft, facing the road and the lake. You can't see Cabin Seven from there."

"My mistake."

"Right." Still smiling, she scooted a little farther away from him, straightening her clothes with hands that were still shaking. "It's been a long day."

He nodded in what might have been resignation. "You're tired."

"Yes. And I don't exactly trust my judgment at the moment. Because, to be perfectly honest, there's nothing I'd like more than to check out the view from the upstairs window with you right now."

His eyes heated and he moved reflexively toward her. She held up a hand and he went still.

"I've known you two days," she reminded him, finding it a little hard to believe, herself, that so little time had passed since she'd thrown herself at him at the gas pump. "And today has been fairly emotional, so I'm not sure how much that's influencing my thinking."

"Then you should go. I wouldn't want to be accused of taking advantage of you." His smile was a little strained, but understanding.

She lifted an eyebrow. "Maybe I would be taking advantage of you. I could be just using you as a tension reliever."

He nodded gravely and spread his hands as if in surrender to her. "I think I'm up to it."

She laughed and punched his shoulder. Leaving him rubbing the spot ruefully, she stood. "I'm going."

He caught up with her at the door, snagged her around the waist and brought her against him again for one more lingering kiss. He held her closely enough to let her know that he was still aroused, but he made no effort to convince her to stay. "Just wanted to give you a little more to think about tonight," he murmured when he finally released her.

As if she didn't already have enough. With a sigh and a shake of her head, she let herself out the door.

She glanced instinctively at the cabin next door when she walked to the golf cart. She saw the blinds in the front window move and, just for the heck of it, she waved. The slats fell abruptly into place and went still.

She really didn't believe any longer that the odd Terrence Landon was a criminal mastermind who needed to be watched furtively from Aaron's cabin. The guy was just too bizarre, she thought as she spun the golf cart out of the driveway and head toward home. But maybe she wouldn't tell Aaron just yet that she was abandoning her clever undercover scheme.

"I feel like a damned idiot," Steven complained, glaring down at his immobilized leg. Having been discharged from the hospital Friday morning, he lay stretched out on his mother's couch that afternoon, his injured leg propped on a pillow. The TV remote, a cooler of bottled water and sodas, enough snack foods to feed half a dozen people, his cell phone, laptop computer and an ebook reader were all within easy reach. And he did not look happy, Aaron thought, studying Steven from a nearby chair.

"It was an accident. Could have happened to anyone."

Steven sighed. "That doesn't make me feel any better. I let my attention wander. Stupid."

Aaron took a sip of his bottled water. He doubted there was much he could say to make Steven feel better about being cooped up on his mother's couch while the rest of the family went about the business of running the busy resort. As the weekend began, they were all needed at their posts, so Steven had convinced them he would be fine alone for a few hours. Aaron knew everyone was checking on Steven frequently, but he'd figured he might as well hang around for a while to keep him company. He didn't mind Steven's crankiness. He'd probably be in much the same mood under the same circumstances.

"Sorry," Steven said, shaking his head. "I don't mean to take it out on you."

Aaron shrugged. "Are you hurting? Do you need anything?"

"My head hurts like hell, but it's not time to take anything for the pain. Don't really like that drugged feeling, anyway."

"Same here. But I can get you an over-the-counter painkiller if it would help."

"Thanks, but I'm okay. So I hear you're going to be laying shingles this weekend."

"Yeah. Won't be the first time."

"Bet you didn't come on vacation planning to climb around on a hot roof, though."

"Frankly, I didn't know what I'd be doing here," Aaron admitted. "I left Dallas on an impulse with no plans for how long I'd be staying. Might as well make myself useful while I'm here."

"You've done that. The family's got you right up there on a pedestal with your brother."

Aaron grimaced. "I hope not. That's a hard fall—trust me, I know. I just haven't been here long enough to tick everyone off yet."

"Make a habit of that, do you?"

"You have no idea."

"Yeah, well, maybe you should give me a few tips on how to deal with it. Because I'm about to royally piss off a whole bunch of Bells."

Aaron felt his eyebrows rise. "What are you talking about?"

Steven let his head fall back on the pile of pillows his mother had arranged behind him before reluctantly leaving for the grill. "I can't do it anymore. I thought I could, but I can't."

Aaron sat silently for a few moments, processing Steven's words. "You're leaving the resort?"

Steven nodded. "I've got to. I mean, I'll stay close to my family, I hope, but I can't keep working here the rest of my life like my granddad and dad and my uncle. Maybe I'll come back to it eventually—probably I will—but I have to try something else first."

"Firefighting?"

"Maybe. Maybe the military, if I can't get in to a firefighter program. Just…something different."

Aaron nodded. "I can understand that."

"I figured you would. It's not that I don't love my family. And I know I'm needed here. But—"

"But it's a big world out there and you need to see a little of it," Aaron finished when Steven floundered for words.

"Yeah, something like that."

"They'll understand, Steven."

"They're going to hate it," Steven corrected flatly. "They'll put on brave faces and tell me to go for what I want while they all look worried and sigh a lot. Pop will tell me I'm a damned fool, Mimi will remind me I'm their only grandson. Bryan will start popping ant-acids and Mom will wipe her eyes when she thinks I'm not looking. I'll be the first in four generations to break away. That's a pretty big deal."

Aaron had to concede that was a lot of pressure. He'd found it burdensome enough that his own family worried about him. He'd never wanted to cause them anxiety, he'd just wanted to follow his own path. Steven wanted nothing more. "You have to do what's best for you. Life's too short to spend it wishing you'd made different choices."

"That's what I decided when I woke up in that ambulance yesterday," Steven admitted, slowly rubbing his temples. "It'll be a few weeks before I'm back on my feet. I'll use that time to decide what I want, but I'm giving notice immediately. I'll stay through Labor Day to get through the summer season and give them time to make other arrangements. It'll take me that long to put in applications and whatever else I have to do, anyway. But after that, come what may, I'm out of here."

It felt strange to hear such recognizable sentiments coming from the other man. Rather than admitting exactly how familiar the words sounded, he asked merely, "Headache?"

"Like an elephant stampede in my skull."

"You should take some aspirin and get some rest. I'll get out of your hair. Is there anything you need before I go?"

"I'm good. And, Aaron—"

"Yeah?"

"Thanks for understanding."

Aaron's chuckle held little humor. "I doubt that anyone could understand better. You'll figure it out, Steven. We both will."

Steven nodded, his eyes already closed as Aaron rose and headed quietly for the door.

He had just stepped out onto the front porch when Shelby arrived in one of the ubiquitous green golf carts. She climbed out to greet him, looking pretty and fresh in a cherry-red scoop-necked top and denim shorts. His body reacted immediately to the sight of her, to the remembrance of having his hands on her—a memory that had kept him awake far too long last night. She really did have great legs, he thought, treating himself to one brief, appreciative survey before raising his gaze back to her face.

"How is he?" she asked, nodding toward the house. Did he see an answering awareness of him in her eyes even as she asked about her brother, or was that merely wishful thinking?

"He's napping. Said his head's hurting." Aaron wouldn't mention the conversation he'd just had with her brother, of course. It was up to Steven to tell his family his plans.

"Should I go in?"

"I'd let him sleep. I think he needs some alone time."

"After a night in the hospital being hovered over, I don't doubt that he does. I'll go back to work, then. I assume he'll call if he needs anyone."

"He will. And I'm sure it won't be long before your mom or grandmother feels compelled to check on him. He'll be okay."

"Thanks for sitting with him for a while. It made Mom feel better about leaving him knowing you were here with him."

"You know I like your brother."

She dimpled. "He's a great guy. Don't tell him I said so."

"Your words are safe with me," he promised her. Though she was only teasing, he would add the sentiment to the other confidences that had been entrusted to him in the past couple of days. He was beginning to feel the weight of them.

She glanced at her watch. "I'll pick you up at seven, by the way. Be ready."

"Uh—"

Her smile was almost blinding. "You haven't forgotten our date, have you? This gal doesn't welsh on her bets."

"I wasn't sure it was still on—what with everything that's happened."

"Steven's going to be okay, so there's no reason for us to sit here and stare at him. Don't worry," she added with a saucy wink, "I won't keep you out too late. I know you have to start hammering shingles first thing in the morning."

He wanted to kiss her so badly he could already taste her on his lips. He settled for tracing her smile with the tip of his finger. "You can keep me out as long as you like."

Her smile quivered just a little and the faintest hint of pink swept upward from her throat to her cheeks. He wasn't the only one feeling the heat that had little to do with the summer temperature, he thought in satisfaction before dropping his hand and stepping back. "I'll see you at seven. By the way, what should I wear? Black tie, scuba gear, hazmat suit? It would help to have a clue—though I warn you, I didn't even pack a jacket or tie. I did throw in a nice shirt and pair of slacks."

Her momentary self-consciousness dissolved into a giggle at his whimsical suggestions. "Your shirt and slacks will be fine."

He made a show of wiping his brow in relief. "Nice to know I won't have to scramble to find a tux to rent."

Still smiling, she glanced at the golf cart. "Want a ride back to your cabin?"

"No, thanks. I'll walk."

Nodding, she hopped back into the driver's seat. "See you in a few hours, Aaron."

He watched her buzz away. He couldn't wait to see what she had planned for him that evening.

Shelby was leaving her parents' house at just before seven that evening when she almost bumped into her younger sister, who was on her way in. They paused on the front porch to speak.

"You look nice," Lori said, giving her a once-over.

Shelby lifted an eyebrow humorously. "You don't have to sound so surprised."

"I'm just not used to seeing you in a dress."

A little self-consciously, Shelby smoothed a hand down the front of her sundress, a crisp white cotton printed with colorful, cheery summer flowers. Scooped at the neckline and fitted at the waist, the dress flared out to swish against the tops of her knees when she walked. She wore small gold hoop earrings, a little gold sand-dollar charm on a thin chain around her neck and a slim gold bangle on her right wrist. She'd left her hair loose and curling around her bare shoulders. The outfit was actually casual, but because she spent so much of her life in tees and shorts, she felt dressed up. All of her family had remarked on her appearance when she'd stopped in to see Steven before leaving for her date, and now Lori had followed suit.

"You wear dresses all the time," Shelby grumbled. "How come no one ever makes a big deal out of that?"

Twitching the skirt of her gauzy midcalf dress that faded from a deep graphite at the top to a silvery pearl at the hem, Lori smiled faintly, but didn't answer. Instead, she asked, "Do you have a date this evening?"

"Yes. Aaron and I are going out."

Something flickered in Lori's expression, too fleetingly for Shelby to pin it down. "You have a thing going with Aaron?"

Shelby rolled her eyes. "We're going out to dinner."

"Has he, uh, said anything about—?"

Frowning, Shelby prodded. "About what?"

Lori shook her head abruptly. "Never mind. I'm going in to see Steven for a few minutes, then I'm heading out myself. I have plans with friends."

"I see."

Lori moved past her, reaching for the door. "Have a good time with Aaron. I'll catch you later." She had the door to the house closed between them almost before Shelby could reply.

Shaking her head in bewilderment, Shelby headed for her car. She had a bet to pay off.

Chapter Eight

If Aaron was surprised when Shelby turned her car into the lot of an exclusive country club after driving almost forty minutes from the resort, he kept the reaction to himself. It had been a pleasant drive, with music and lively conversation. Aaron was so easy to talk to, she mused as she drove around the crowded parking lot, searching for an empty slot. From pop culture to politics, they'd swapped opinions and observations, usually agreeing, occasionally differing, but always respectfully. The time had passed so quickly it was almost a surprise to her when she'd reached the club where she'd decided to bring him.

"There's a spot," Aaron said, pointing ahead and to the left.

She turned quickly into the narrow opening. "Whew. I was beginning to think we were going to have to park on the street."

"Looks like there's quite a crowd here this evening. Some kind of event, I take it?"

She nodded. "It's a big charity bash that's been planned for months. The resort bought tickets weeks ago as a donation to the cause, but no one else was interested in attending. I wasn't sure I'd come, until this date bet came up. I figured coming here was a way to pay my debt to you and contribute to the local women and children's shelter at the same time."

Aaron flashed her a smile. "I like that," he said. "So am I dressed okay? It's not a coat and tie event, is it?"

She nodded toward two couples climbing out of a large SUV nearby, both of the women in casual dresses, the men dressed very much like Aaron in dress shirts and chinos, no tie in sight. "Casual dress was encouraged, just no jeans or collarless shirts. That's a club restriction, I think, though I'm not a member."

He reached for his door handle. "Well, then, let's go be charitable."

Sliding out from beneath the wheel, Shelby was pleased that Aaron seemed to approve her choice. She'd spent several hours debating over what they should do this evening—miniature golf? A picnic? Horseback riding? A concert?—but her thoughts had kept coming back to this event organized by a local women's organization in which several of her college sorority friends were active. She'd considered joining, herself, but her work at the resort kept her so busy during the summers, in addition to her few outside civic activities, that she wasn't sure she had enough spare time to contribute. Maybe tonight would change her mind.

She and Aaron met up at the back of her car and he held out his arm, smiling down at her. "Have I told you how pretty you look tonight?"

"You have," she replied with an answering smile. "Thank you again."

"My pleasure."

He looked quite delectable himself, in his pale blue shirt and gray slacks. He'd combed his dark hair neatly, but a rebellious lock still tumbled onto his forehead, almost begging her to reach up and smooth it back. She resisted only because it looked so appealing exactly the way it fell.

"Am I going to run into more strangers who tell me how happy they are to see me again?" he asked as they approached the entrance doors just behind the two couples from the SUV.

She tried to remember if any of the friends she would encounter inside had met Andrew. "I don't think so."

He nodded and held the door for her. "That's a relief."

She handed their tickets to the host inside the impressive lobby of the venerable establishment. Despite the rather stuffy decor, the noise level was high and a little rowdy, with laughter, conversation and music spilling out of several of the rooms around them. The whole place had been reserved for the event, and according to the program they were given, there were plenty of activities to entertain them: a casino room where they could win tickets for prizes. A karaoke bar. Dancing to a live band in the main ballroom. And plenty of food, from buffalo wings to a sushi bar.

"Doesn't look like we're going to be bored," she commented, perusing the options with a lifted eyebrow.

Aaron put a hand at the back of her waist. "I've yet to be bored with you," he murmured.

Her flattered response to the rather casual compliment seemed out of proportion. Was she really still stinging over Pete's loss of interest in her, even as she

herself had given up on them as a couple? *Pathetic,
Shelby.*

Aaron was either the most accomplished actor she'd
ever met or perhaps the most well-trained gentleman, or
maybe both. Or maybe he really did have a good time
with her that evening. His smiles and laughs certainly
seemed genuine. They ate, played at the casino games
and competed fiercely to see who could win the most
tickets. They even sang karaoke—and while Shelby
considered herself a decent vocalist, she was not particularly surprised to discover that Aaron was even better. He had a very nice, deep voice with a sexy Texas
drawl that was well suited to the heartbroken-cowboy
song he selected.

She couldn't help being proud to be seen with him,
to introduce him to her old friends who didn't often
see her out with such dashing companions. They had
grown accustomed to her comfortably sedate relationship with Pete, and she'd been grumpily aware of the
pitying looks she'd received from a few of them since
the breakup, but they were obviously intrigued to see
her with Aaron. Her feminine pride couldn't help but
be bolstered.

"You have a beautiful voice," she said to him when
they two-stepped to the music of a country-western
band in the ballroom later. "Have you ever performed
professionally?"

He shook his head. "Lots of family sing-alongs
around campfires at my uncle's ranch. Took choir in
high school for an easy A."

She laughed and confessed, "Me, too. Turned out it
was way harder than I expected. My choir teacher was
tough. I had to work harder than I'd expected for that
A, but I enjoyed it."

He twirled her, then brought her back into his hold. "Once we've enjoyed another dance or two, we should head back into the casino room. I think you're still ahead of me by a couple of tickets. Can't have that."

She laughed. "You are so competitive."

His grin flashed. "Says the pot to the kettle."

"*Moi?* How silly. Although I believe I do have a few more tickets than you."

Chuckling, he spun her again as the song came to an end. She stumbled when she came face-to-face with Pete.

"Hello, Shelby."

She gave a strained smile to the tall, auburn-haired man who had moved to stand in front of her on the dance floor. "Hi, Pete. I didn't expect to see you here."

She had met twenty-seven-year-old accountant Pete Van Pelt at a meeting of a local CPA organization almost two years ago. She rarely attended meetings with the group now, mostly because she had no particular career ambitions outside the resort, so she hadn't seen Pete since their breakup several months earlier. She knew he didn't particularly like crowds or parties, but because he did have professional aspirations, she supposed he'd thought this was a good chance to network and be seen as a community volunteer.

"Laura Granderson invited me. It's a good cause, so I thought I'd make an appearance."

He looked at Aaron then. "I have to confess I'm surprised to see you here, Andrew."

Aaron looked at Shelby with a questioning expression. She smiled wryly and drew him forward. "Aaron, this is Pete Van Pelt. Pete, this is Andrew's brother, Aaron Walker. He's been staying at the resort this week for a vacation."

The men shook hands. Though she suspected he'd recognized the name, Aaron greeted Pete with the same courtesy he'd shown everyone else. To give him credit, Pete didn't exclaim about Aaron's resemblance to Andrew, merely apologized politely for mistaking him for his brother.

"You look very nice tonight," Pete said, eying Shelby's dress and strappy sandals. He probably noticed that she'd even gone to the extra effort of polishing her toenails a bright hot pink; Pete didn't miss that sort of detail. He had the courtesy not to point out, as Lori had, that she was rarely seen in a dress, but she'd bet he was thinking something along that line.

Aaron moved closer to her side, resting a hand on her back. "Excuse us, Pete. We were just going to try out some more of the casino games. It was nice to meet you."

"Yeah, you, too, Aaron. So, you're just here through the weekend?"

Aaron smiled intimately down at Shelby. "That's still up for consideration."

Pete looked somberly from one of them to the other. "I see. Well, have a good time, you two."

Though she didn't look back, Shelby had the sensation that Pete watched them as they moved toward the doorway.

Shelby parked in front of Cabin Eight later that evening, cut the engine and turned off the headlights. It was well after ten, but she was in no hurry to leave. The night had been almost magical so far, and she wasn't ready for it to end.

"I had the best time tonight," she said, fingering the wooden bracelet on her arm that would serve as a me-

mento of the evening. Some very nice items had been donated for door prizes—redeemable with tickets from the casino games—and she'd won this bangle donated by a local woodworking artist. Aaron's prize had been a football autographed by last year's Texas Longhorns team and coach. He'd seemed pleased, commenting to Shelby that he had a young cousin who would be thrilled to receive it. Both of them had made donations to the charity before leaving the event.

Aaron tossed the football from one hand to another. "It was fun. You did good picking the evening's entertainment. Food, games, singing, dancing…a little taste of everything."

She smiled. "That was clever of me, wasn't it? And all for a good cause."

"Would you like to come in for a nightcap? And by nightcap, I mean a light beer or a cup of tea, the only things I have to offer."

"Tea sounds good."

Cabin Seven was dark and would have looked deserted had it not been for the car still parked in the drive. Shelby spared only a glance next door as she followed Aaron into Cabin Eight.

He closed the door behind them. He'd left only a lamp burning, so the main room was intimately dim. Dropping the football onto a chair, he turned to face her without turning on the overhead light. With his back to the lamp, his face was in shadow, the expression in his dark eyes hidden, though she thought she saw them glitter. She swallowed hard, pushing her suddenly damp palms down her thighs.

His voice was husky when he asked, "Beer or tea?"

"I'm…not really thirsty," she admitted, the slight

pause giving her a moment to decide whether she really wanted to do this.

She did.

Taking a step toward him, she murmured, "Are you still interested in showing me the view from your bedroom window?"

"Oh, yeah," he rasped out.

He stood very still, letting her make the moves. Confident now, she laid her palms on his chest and rose on tiptoe to take a taste of his mouth. He rested his hands on her hips. She felt the impatience quivering in his muscles, but still he held back. Sliding her hands slowly up his chest, she kissed him again, a little harder this time, nipping at his lower lip until she elicited a low moan of response from him. "Aaron?"

He brushed his mouth across hers. "Mmm?"

"Either we go upstairs now, or I'm going to drag you right down to the rug beneath our feet."

His laugh sounded a lot like a groan. Taking a step backward, he held out a hand to her, and she laid hers in it. They turned together toward the stairs.

Minutes later, her pretty dress was a colorful puddle on the hardwood floor beside the bed. His shirt lay close to her dress, while his pants were draped half on, half off the little chair nearby. He tossed her lace bra in the general direction of the rest of the clothes. She didn't know where it landed, but she'd worry about that later.

Finally, they were skin to skin. And it was every bit as delicious as she'd fantasized. She'd seen his bare chest before, during their water outing, and she had admired it then. Now she had time for a leisurely examination, using her eyes, her hands, her lips. The bedside lamp was dimmed so that the light glowed softly on his sleek skin, illuminating her path as she kissed a line from the hollow of his throat to his shallow navel. Her hand slid downward, seeking, stroking, cupping, and the groan she ripped from his throat was immensely satisfying.

His fortitude weakening, he tugged at her shoulders, lifting her upward, flipping her over so that he could do a little exploring of his own. His hands sought her breasts—and while she'd always thought they were on the small side, Aaron seemed more than satisfied when he rubbed her nipples into tight points, then lowered his head to taste them. She gasped and arched, offering more. He accepted that invitation eagerly.

She would have liked to take the time to study and taste every inch of Aaron's hard body, and he muttered that he wanted to do the same with her. It turned out neither of them had the patience.

"I need to be inside you," he grated, every inch of him quivering with fiercely harnessed restraint.

Barely coherent, she whispered, "I need you there."

He took care of protection swiftly, efficiently, then returned to hold himself over her, one hand gently touching her face. "You're sure?"

Touched by her utter confidence that he would stop if she said the word, despite his very obvious hunger for more, she traced his lips with one fingertip before answering. Images of the time they'd spent together flashed through her mind—such a short time, in actuality, but packed so full. During these past few days, she had learned that he was kind, generous, fun, adventurous, talented, a little rebellious—not to mention drop-dead sexy. How could she not have fallen for him? How could she hold him at a distance, even though she was convinced she would be nursing a broken heart for quite a long while after he left?

"Shelby?"

Forcing a smile, she slid a hand to the back of his neck and drew his mouth to hers. "I'm sure," she murmured against his lips.

His exultant thrust forward made her concerns about the future dissolve in a haze of passion, took away her ability even to form a coherent thought. She wrapped her legs around him, buried her fingers in his hair and opened her mouth to his demanding tongue. For now, he was hers. The future would take care of itself.

Wearing only a pair of khaki shorts, and those unbuttoned at the waist, Aaron lounged on the bed and watched as Shelby wriggled into her slightly wrinkled dress. She winced as she reached back to struggle with the zipper. "Aren't you going to offer to help?"

His hair tumbling appealingly into his eyes, he gave her a lopsided grin. "I prefer getting you out of your clothes."

Still, he pushed off the mattress and moved to stand behind her, slowly raising the zipper while she held her hair out of the way. He finished with a lingering kiss on her nape that made her shiver. Letting her hair fall, she moved away from him with determination. "Don't start that again or we'll be climbing back into bed."

His grin deepening, he reached for her, but she eluded him skillfully, holding up both hands with a breathless laugh. "Aaron."

Sighing loudly, he stopped. "Okay, fine. Go."

"It's already after midnight. You told Uncle Bryan you'd meet him at seven to start roofing before it gets too hot. You need to get some rest first. Trust me, he's a hard taskmaster."

"That doesn't surprise me. I can handle it."

Smiling, she reached out to touch his cheek. "I have no doubt."

Catching her hand, he placed a kiss in her palm, then closed her fingers around it and led her toward the stairs.

She turned to him at the door, smiling up at him. "It was a wonderful evening, Aaron. Every minute of it."

"For me, too," he assured her.

Tilting her head, she studied his expression. "You really enjoyed the charity thing? Some people might have thought it was a little cheesy. You know, casino games and karaoke."

"Like your old buddy Pete?" He chuckled. "The guy looked like he'd rather be just about anywhere else, but was putting on a good face for some reason."

"For career reasons," she informed him. "Pete is all about the networking."

"Well, I thought it was fun. Your friends did a great job putting it all together, and I'm sure they made a tidy sum for the charity."

"And," she reminded him with a grin, "I paid off my debt. Next challenge we make, I expect to win."

"You're on."

She reached for the doorknob, knowing if she didn't leave now, she would be too tempted to stay.

He followed her to stand in the open doorway when she stepped out onto the porch. At this late hour, the area was mostly quiet—partially because resort rules required courtesy to other guests after 10:00 p.m. The sounds of only a few voices and car engines drifted their way over the frogs, insects, lapping water and other familiar outdoor night noises.

"There was one thing Pete did seem to appreciate tonight." Though he spoke quietly, lightly, he didn't seem particularly amused. "He couldn't take his eyes off you."

She laughed skeptically. "Even if that was true, it would probably be because he didn't expect to see me there, especially with you."

Knowing Pete, he would wonder what Aaron saw in her—or if Aaron, too, considered her to be a great "pal" with whom to spend a pleasant evening.

"More likely because he was wishing you were there with him instead of me."

Aaron's rather grumpy comment made her raise her eyebrows. If she didn't know better, she would think he actually sounded a little jealous. Which, of course, was ridiculous.

"Save the performance for the family," she teased him. She wanted to make it very clear that she wasn't expecting anything after their lovemaking tonight. From the start, it had been important to her to hold on to her pride during this...whatever it was between them. "You can flirt with me in front of them tomorrow, and I'll be suitably flattered. And then when I eventually, very politely and somewhat regretfully dash your hopes, they'll be even more convinced that I'm not trying desperately to catch a man."

Though his answering smile looked a little forced, she told herself she'd struck the right note. If Aaron was worried that she would make it awkward for him to leave when he decided it was time, she wanted to re-assure him she would not. Just as Andrew had driven away with a friendly, standing invitation to return any time he liked, she wanted Aaron to always feel welcome here. By all of them. If she had a few pangs about wishing things were different, that he could be more than a long-distance friend who popped in and out of her life occasionally—well, no one needed to know that. Especially him.

Both of them jumped when a car door slammed unexpectedly in the next driveway. Shelby hadn't seen anyone get into the vehicle, but she'd been looking at Aaron. She doubted that he'd gotten a look at the driver, either, before the car backed out of the drive and sped away faster than the posted resort speed limits would have sanctioned. She looked at the front door of Cabin Seven, thinking she might see Terrence Landon, but the door was closed. There was no way to know if he'd seen her and Aaron.

She glanced at Aaron, who gave her a wry shrug, which she returned. Getting into her own car more quietly than the other driver, she made the very short drive home, noting in relief that all the windows were darkened in the family houses she passed. It wasn't that she owed any explanations for where she'd been or what she'd done, but some things just needed to remain private. Privacy was in short supply here in the family compound, she thought wryly. It was something she'd accepted when she'd made the decision that she wanted to work in the family business. Maybe someday she would get a place outside the resort and drive in to work every day, as Hannah had done when she'd been married to the evil ex, but for now Shelby was content where she was. Even if she had to sneak into her trailer at nearly 1:00 a.m. just to avoid those knowing looks tomorrow, she thought, doing just that.

She didn't expect to get much sleep that night, but she didn't mind. She would be quite content to lie nestled in her bed, the extra pillow cuddled in her arms, a blissful smile on her face as she drifted in replays of the most perfect night of her life. No thoughts of the past or future allowed, just a mental replay of every touch, every kiss, every husky groan. Even if she never had the pleasure of making love with Aaron again, she would commit each one of those precious moments to her memory.

Aaron was half surprised that he didn't smash his thumb with a hammer sometime before lunch on Saturday. As experienced as he was at laying shingles and driving nails, his inability to direct his entire attention to the task put his digits at risk more than once. Fortunately, he was able to hide his concentration issues from his boss for the day. Bryan Bell seemed satisfied with Aaron's work as the morning progressed.

The roof decking was in good shape, so the prep work went fairly quickly. Cabins One, Two and Three were all standard truss-roof construction, which were easier to reshingle than the A-frames closer to the lake. When Aaron offered initially to be the one climbing around on the roof, Bryan set him straight quickly enough. "I'm fifty-three, boy, not a hundred," he said flatly. "We just got Dad to quit climbing up on roofs last year, when he turned eighty."

Aaron smiled apologetically. "I wasn't implying that you were too old to be up here. Just volunteering to do the grunt work."

Bryan dropped a heavy bundle of asphalt shingles on the roof and pulled his hammer out of his tool belt. "I've been doing grunt work around here since the place opened when I was in junior high. Never wanted to do anything else."

Nodding, Aaron ripped the wrapping off the shingles and got to work, trying to focus on anything other than his complicated feelings about Shelby. It helped that he and Bryan talked easily while they worked, mostly about fishing and hunting in east Texas, two of Bryan's favorite hobbies. The resort was busy on this nice Saturday, and the sounds of voices, cars and boat motors underlay their conversation, but Cabin Two was in a somewhat secluded spot across from the motel, not on the water, so they were able to work in relative privacy. From the rooftop Aaron had a good view of the pool and the fishing pier, both of which were popular that morning.

Bryan didn't bring up Shelby's name, nor did Aaron, even though she was never far from his thoughts. He kept mentally replaying her cheery comments about her plan to "politely" and "somewhat regretfully" shoot him down to convince her family she wasn't looking for a man. He'd tried for the rest of the night to convince himself that he was relieved she felt that way, that he certainly wasn't on the market for anything more, himself, that he'd be a fool not to appreciate the no-strings-attached vacation fling Shelby seemed to be offering. Exactly what he wanted. Right?

Which didn't explain why he'd punched his pillow a few times during the night as if blaming it for his inability to sleep.

It was just after one o'clock that afternoon when Bryan looked toward the main road and grunted. "That's Lori's car. Looks like she's just getting home from last night. She tells her folks she's staying with friends from college, but..." He shrugged.

Because he was pretty sure he knew exactly whom Lori had spent the night with, Aaron kept his mouth shut.

"Listen to me, gossiping like an old hen," Bryan said with a rueful grunt. "Guess you're just an easy man to talk to. But considering Hannah's situation, I'm hardly one to talk about my brother's kids."

Figuring the older man was referring to his daughter's ill-fated marriage and ugly divorce, Aaron stuck with his no-comment policy, merely reaching for another shingle. He certainly didn't want to encourage the conversation to wind around to where Shelby had spent most of the night.

Bryan stood and pressed a hand to his back while wiping his dripping forehead with his other arm. "I need a break. Let's go get some lunch. Sarah said she'd have food ready for us when we got hungry."

They'd been working steadily since a twenty-minute restroom, shade and water break at ten, and both of them were flagging. Pop had been by a couple of times to "supervise" and offer his help, but Bryan had sent him on his way. Maggie had brought cold bottles of water several times, but had been too busy with her own chores to linger, and everyone else was occupied with the weekend rush.

Leaving their tools safely stashed, they climbed down from the roof and headed for the marina building, stopping in the restroom to wash up before eating. Even after washing, Aaron felt grubby in his sweat-stained T-shirt and dirty-kneed jeans, his hair damp and cap-creased. Still, he was surprised to find himself the target of several disapproving frowns from various members of the Bell family when he walked into the grill.

Did he look that bad? He resisted an urge to sniff his own shirt. He was used to being greeted with almost overwhelming enthusiasm by these people. The chill he sensed now took him aback.

Maybe they had somehow figured out what had taken place between him and Shelby last night and were expressing their disapproval. Despite her claims that her family had no say in her social life, perhaps a cabin in the heart of the resort hadn't been the best place for them to have their first intimate encounter.

Taking a quick headcount, he saw that the frowns were coming from Shelby's parents, her grandmother and her aunt. Bryan looked a bit baffled. No one from the younger generation was present at the moment.

Because it would look questionable to turn and bolt now, he proceeded into the grill, taking an empty seat at a table next to Bryan.

"Hi, everyone," he said.

C.J. studied him from over the tops of his glasses. "I understand you've been talking with my son."

Caught off guard by this comment he hadn't expected, Aaron said, "I've spent some time with Steven while I've been here. Sat with him for a while yesterday. Why?"

Sarah cleared her throat and Aaron noticed only then that her eyes looked a bit red-rimmed. "Steven told us this morning that he's leaving the resort as soon as his leg is healed. He's talking about training to fight wildfires, or—" she had to swallow before finishing "—or maybe joining the military."

"Yes, he mentioned that to me," Aaron admitted.

"And you encouraged him?" C.J. demanded.

"I neither encouraged nor discouraged him. Not my place. I simply listened."

Sarah spoke again. "When I pointed out to him that you work for your family, he corrected me. He said you aren't working for anyone at the moment. He implied that you don't think working for family is a good idea."

"I didn't say that, either," Aaron replied, keeping a firm grip on his patience. He would not get defensive, he promised himself. He understood that the family was still in shock over Steven's announcement, especially coming so soon after the accident in which they could have lost him permanently. "I'm simply not interested in the investigation and security business. It mostly involves sitting behind a computer or in endless meetings or business presentations, and that just doesn't appeal to me. Unlike Andrew, I'm not the big-desk-in-a-corner-office type. Doesn't mean I think it's a bad idea, just that it's not something I aspire to. I'm sure Steven's given a lot of thought to the type of career he wants to pursue."

He didn't know when Shelby had entered the diner behind him, but when she spoke, he figured she'd heard at least part of his explanation.

"Would everyone please stop glaring at Aaron?" she demanded in exasperation. "He had nothing to do with Steven's decision to find another job. We've all known for some time that Steven was getting restless, long before Aaron showed up here."

"Well, of course you would defend Aaron," Mimi murmured, looking archly from him to Shelby. "As much time as you've been spending with him this week."

Thinking of the most recent time he'd spent with her, Aaron studiously avoided looking toward Shelby.

"What's everyone doing in here?" Lori wandered in, looking as carefully put together as always, even on a Saturday afternoon, in a see-through shades-of-gray-swirled top over a darker gray camisole and gray linen pants. Both her fingernails and the toenails revealed by her black sandals were painted silver. "Why do you all look so serious?"

The family spun to look at their youngest member,

and Aaron was briefly relieved that the attention had turned from him. His relief was short-lived.

"Have you been seeing that Webber boy again?" C.J. demanded of Lori. "After we made it very clear that you should steer clear of that troublemaker?"

Lori whirled toward Aaron, her expression stormy. "You *told* them?"

He winced when all eyes focused on him, again with palpable disapproval. "I didn't say anything," he assured Lori in a mumble.

"Eileen Copping saw you making out with that boy at the burger drive-in last night," Mimi said with a touch of smugness that she was the one who'd reported Lori's misbehavior. "She called me this morning, and of course I felt obligated to tell your parents."

Sarah glanced at the few other diners in the place before looking at her younger daughter. "We'll discuss this with you later," she said in a low voice.

Lori tossed her head defiantly. "You can say anything you want, but I won't stop seeing Zach just because none of you like him."

With that pronouncement, she turned and stalked out of the diner without looking back. After which everyone turned back to Aaron. He cleared his throat.

"You knew Lori was seeing Zach?" C.J. asked in disbelief.

"I didn't know his name," Aaron countered. "I ran into the two of them in town one day and she asked me not to mention that I'd seen her. Because it was none of my business, I agreed."

"Humph." Mimi gave him a stern shake of her finger. "You should have figured out when she asked you not to say anything that she was up to something. That right there was your clue that you shouldn't have agreed."

"Mimi, it wasn't Aaron's responsibility to tattle on Lori to the family," Shelby said in exasperation, plopping in the chair beside him as if to solidify her endorsement. "You're being unfair."

"I'm going to have to side with Shelby on this one," Bryan declared. "Aaron doesn't want to get in the middle here. Now, how about feeding the boy? He's been up on the roof of Cabin Two all morning in the heat helping me with the shingles."

Grateful for the support, Aaron nodded slightly to Bryan and patted Shelby's leg beneath the table. She covered his hand with her and gave a little squeeze.

She looked nice today, he thought fleetingly. She wore a pastel-plaid tailored top with cap sleeves, sand-colored jeans and green flats rather than her usual shorts. Though he had to admit he missed seeing her legs.

"I'm sorry, Aaron," Sarah said contritely, drawing his attention away from Shelby. "They're right, we shouldn't be ganging up on you this way. I'll get your lunch."

He supposed he'd made a convenient target, especially since he'd actually been privy to the secrets of both Lori and Steven. As for his relationship with Shelby—well, they'd really be giving him the stink eye if they knew all *those* details.

Though the mood was still somewhat more subdued than usual, they finished the lunch break civilly enough. That was mostly thanks to Shelby, who kept the conversation moving with determination, barely stopping to breathe as she chattered about last night's charity event, about the mutual acquaintances she had seen there, about the money raised for a charity they all supported and about how grateful the event's organizers had been for the donation made by the Bell Resort.

Before long, Bryan glanced at his watch. "Ready to get back to it, Aaron? I figure we can put in another two or three hours today, then finish up tomorrow."

Aaron nodded. "I'm ready."

At least Bryan seemed to have no issues with him, which made Aaron glad he didn't know any secrets about either of Bryan's daughters.

Sarah carried a take-out bag to the table and handed it to Shelby. "Would you take this over to Steven, please? Tell him I'll come by before the dinner rush to check on him."

Shelby rose and walked out with Aaron. He lingered for a few moments with her outside the building, telling Bryan he'd meet him at the cabin.

"I think I'm in trouble," he said, making a show of wiping his brow. "Uh—Minnesota."

Though she laughed ruefully in response to his silly code word, Shelby grimaced. "They're just mad at Steven and Lori and taking it out on you. I'm sorry."

"It's okay. Parents tend to worry about their kids, no matter how old the kids get. Not to mention that Steven's going to be hard to replace around here."

Shelby nodded, her throat moving with a swallow. "But he deserves a chance to follow his dreams," she said firmly. "Even if those dreams take him into situations that scare the stuffing out of those of us who love him."

"Your brother will be fine, Shelby."

She sighed lightly. "I know you can't guarantee that. But thanks for the reassurance."

"Lori will be okay, too. She's really not a child, you know."

Shelby placed a hand on the back of her neck, beneath her hair, as if the muscles in her neck had tightened again. "Zach Webber is bad news. Trust me, Lori would be better off listening to Mom and Dad this time. I think she's only using him as another one of her mini rebellions."

Remembering the intensity he'd sensed between Lori and Zach, Aaron wasn't so sure. But again—none of his business.

"Guess I'd better get back on that roof."

Shelby nodded and dropped her hand, lifting the other to display the take-out bag. "And I'd better deliver this to Steven before it gets cold. I'll see you later?"

"I'd like that."

They both started to turn away, then paused when someone called out Shelby's name.

Aaron was not particularly happy to see Pete Van Pelt hurrying toward them from the parking lot, looking much more casual today in a polo shirt and jeans. He smiled broadly at Shelby, ignoring Aaron for the moment. "Hi, Shel," he said.

"Pete, what are you doing here?"

"It's such a nice day, I decided to take a drive, maybe enjoy a slice of one of your mom's delicious pies. I hoped I'd run into you, have a chance to say hello. You look very nice, by the way."

"Thanks, Pete, but I'm afraid I have to run," she said, slanting a slightly baffled look at Aaron. "I'm delivering lunch to my brother. He was hurt a couple days ago, and he's going to be laid up for a few weeks."

"I'm sorry to hear that. Is he up to having company? I could accompany you, give him my regards."

"Oh." She shuffled her weight a bit, then shrugged.

"Sure, come on. We can take one of the carts. I'm sure he'd enjoy the company."

"Nice to see you again, Aaron," Pete added, as if belatedly remembering his manners.

"You, too, Pete. Now if you'll excuse me. Later, Shelby."

He turned and moved quickly toward the cabin, his mood considerably dimmed from only a few minutes earlier.

Chapter Nine

Aaron looked as though he'd just climbed out of the shower when he answered the door in response to Shelby's light knock that evening. His hair was wet and his white T-shirt clung to his damp chest. Beneath the hem of his loose jeans, his feet were bare.

"I hope you haven't eaten yet," she said, hearing the slight breathiness of her own voice but hoping he hadn't noticed. She slid the strap of an insulated tote bag off her shoulder. "I brought food."

He hesitated for a moment, then moved out of the doorway and motioned her inside. "As a matter of fact, I haven't eaten. And I'm starving."

"I thought you might be after that day of manual labor." She carried the tote to the bar.

"Have to admit I haven't worked that hard in a while," he said, placing a hand to his back as if to press against the kinks there. "And the worst part? Your uncle has twenty-three years on me and he still worked circles around me."

She laughed. "We've always said Uncle Bryan's like that windup bunny on TV. He never runs out of energy. Dad has always been content to work the marina, but Bryan has to be all over the resort doing a little bit of everything."

"I thought maybe you'd have other plans tonight," he said as he opened a cabinet and took down a couple of plates.

"Other plans? No. You and I mentioned having dinner together again this evening."

"Well, yes. But that was before your boyfriend showed up this afternoon."

She paused with one hand inside the tote bag, her jaw almost dropping in surprise at his tone. She must have been mistaken, she told herself with a slight shake of her head. After all, Aaron wasn't invested enough in this temporary alliance to be jealous, was he?

"Pete?" she asked, though she knew exactly whom he meant. "Yes, that was odd that he came by today. Last night was the first time I'd seen him in months. I suppose that made him think about driving out today to see everyone."

"To see *you*." He stressed the distinction.

"Maybe," she admitted. "I guess he was curious about what I've been up to since we broke up. I know he asked a few questions about you—how long I've known you, whether we've been dating, that sort of thing."

Setting forks beside the plates, Aaron reached for drinking glasses to fill with ice. "Looked to me like he wants you back."

"He's the one who broke it off," she said with a shrug.

"So he's changed his mind. Maybe seeing you with someone else woke him up to what he was missing."

The thought had crossed her mind that Pete's interest in her had been renewed after seeing her with another man—a very handsome and dashing other man, at that. Pete had tried flirting a little that afternoon, but she'd kept her own responses strictly friendly, sharing impersonal small talk in the golf cart, focusing on Steven during their short visit with him, then sending Pete on his way afterward by telling him it had been nice to see him, but she had to get back to work.

"Maybe we'll talk later?" he had asked.

"Sure," she'd said breezily. "I'll give you a call sometime."

After searching her face for a moment, he'd left. She hoped he'd figured out that the chances of her calling him were very slim, despite her polite prevarication.

"I don't know what Pete was thinking when he showed up today," she said to Aaron, "but I think I made it clear to him that I'm not interested in getting involved with him again. He's a nice enough guy, but whatever we had is over and I have no interest in trying to revive it. It would only end the same way, if not worse."

From inside the open fridge, Aaron muttered something she couldn't quite understand. He emerged with a pitcher of tea and deliberately changed the subject. "So, how's Steven feeling?"

"Better. He's getting impatient to be back on his feet. He's already researching the steps he'll need to take to sign up for firefighter training. That's his first choice for a career. I think he just mentions the military as a way of making firefighting sound more acceptable to Mom," she added with a short laugh.

"He'll get there. He's wanted it too long not to give it everything he's got to attain it."

She nodded. "I just didn't realize quite how much he wanted it. His brush with disaster must have really solidified that desire for him. He told me he still feels guilty about running out on the family, but I encouraged him to go after what he wants. It's not like we can't hire a replacement for him. We get job applications all the time."

"I'm sure you do. It's hard work, but it's a great life for someone who doesn't want to be tied to a desk from nine to five, who likes working with his hands and being around lots of people, who appreciates being out in nature."

"Yes, it is." She opened a container of food and set it within easy reach on the bar.

They talked about inconsequential things while they ate roasted chicken sandwiches and pita chips with artichoke hummus that Shelby had made herself. Steering their conversation away from her family issues—specifically, the annoying way her parents had turned on him earlier—Shelby kept him talking about his own interesting family. He told her stories about visiting his uncle Jared's ranch, which had served as a foster home for at-risk boys for quite a few years. Aaron said he'd long since lost count of the number of boys who'd called the ranch home, even for a short time, but he added that most of them had grown into grateful, respectable men who stayed in contact with the family. He had many amusing anecdotes to tell about the ranch, some of which included the notorious "terrible trio."

"I just love hearing about Andrew getting into those scrapes," she admitted, laughing as they cleared away the dinner plates. "It's so hard to picture him being a little wild and crazy."

"It certainly is these days."

Apparently he didn't want to talk about his twin. He moved toward the living room. "Want to watch a movie or something? I wouldn't mind putting my feet up for a couple hours."

"We could watch a movie—or there's a Rangers game."

His smile was almost blinding. "I knew there was a reason I like you."

"Prepare to love me," she shot back with a grin. "I brought popcorn. Have a seat on the couch and turn on the TV, I'll fire up the microwave."

"You just stole my heart," he assured her gravely, his dark eyes dancing.

Though they were only teasing, she still had to swallow a tiny sigh as she moved past him to pull bags of popcorn out of the tote she'd brought with her.

It was almost a perfect evening, she thought later. With the lights dimmed, they snuggled together on the couch with bowls of popcorn and bottles of cold beer, talking about nothing more momentous than the action on the television screen. When they finished the snacks, Aaron wrapped an arm around her shoulder and she laid her head on his chest. She didn't actually doze, but she drifted in a haze of contentment, enjoying every moment, refusing to think beyond the ninth inning.

It was dark outside when Aaron walked into the kitchen for a glass of water. He paused, looking out the little window over the sink. "In the mood for a walk?"

"Why?"

"My neighbor just drove away. How about if you and I take a little moonlight stroll?"

"Sure." She stood and slid her feet into the green flats she'd kicked off earlier. "Are we going to snoop through his cabin?"

He chuckled. "How can you make breaking and entering sound like such a perfectly logical idea?"

"It's not really breaking and entering. I have a master key and as management, I can legally enter any rented unit on the premises if I have reason to do so. Like, maybe, thinking I smell smoke. I can't touch the belongings of the guest," she admitted, "but I could certainly do an inspection."

"For now, let's just look around outside a little," he suggested, moving toward the back door.

She followed cooperatively, though she made sure her keys were in her pocket when she stepped outside.

Glancing around when he closed the door behind them, he reached out to take her hand. She didn't see anyone around to observe them, but she curled her fingers around his and tried to look casual, anyway, like someone simply out enjoying the mild evening with a handsome man. A boat passed on the lake, running lights flashing on the water, the scent of exhaust lingering in the air behind it. The wake stirred up low waves that splashed against the pebbled shoreline. It was just here, Shelby remembered, that she'd competed against Aaron skipping rocks. Right at this spot when he'd kissed her senseless afterward. Had that really been only three nights ago?

Turning her so that her back was to Landon's cabin, Aaron wrapped his arms around her and rested his cheek against her hair. "The place definitely looks unoccupied," he murmured, gazing toward the cabin.

It was hard to think about spying on Landon when she was standing in Aaron's arms in the moonlight, she thought wistfully. Still, she cleared her throat and said softly, "Maybe we could sneak onto the porch and find out if we can see anything through the glass door. Maybe he left a crack in the blinds."

Aaron didn't say anything for a minute and she thought he was going to tell her that was a terrible idea. But then he surprised her by nodding. "What the heck. We aren't going in," he added quickly. "Not without a good reason. But it wouldn't hurt to take a glance inside. You said housekeeping hasn't been inside in a week. You should probably make sure he hasn't trashed the place."

"Do you think he's gone for good? He hasn't been leaving at night, has he?"

"He hasn't left at all while I've been here. I guess it's possible he's slipped out. Has he paid his bill?"

"He paid in cash through next Wednesday. If he's gone, he didn't leave owing us anything."

"Let's go see. But first…" He tipped her chin up so that he could press a lingering kiss to her lips.

Shelby wound her arms around his neck and kissed him back with enough enthusiasm that he seemed to forget the reason they were out, at least for a few heated minutes. When he finally lifted his head, he looked down at her with eyes that glittered hungrily in the moonlight. "Maybe we should forget about Landon and just go back inside."

Delighted with the rush of feminine power that accompanied his dazed expression, she laughed. "We'll just stop for a quick look at Cabin Seven on the way."

He sighed heavily. "Okay. Fine. Let's hurry."

So maybe it would last only another few days. Maybe hours. She was going to enjoy him while she had him.

Moving somewhat furtively, they paused in the shadows near the back entrance to Landon's cabin. "I'll keep watch," Aaron said. "As sketchy as it is for you to look inside, there's no justification at all for me to do so. Look in the back door and windows, see if anything looks sketchy to you."

"And if I don't see anything?" She reached into her pocket and rattled the keys. "Should I go in, take a look around? I wouldn't touch anything that belongs to him, but I could always claim I thought I smelled smoke."

He frowned as if in consideration. "Maybe you should check what you can see through the glass first."

Nodding, she moved onto the porch to look, staying in shadow as much as possible. For once, she was not comforted by the excellent security lighting around the resort.

Landon had left the blinds tightly closed in the cabin's back windows. But there was enough of a gap in the vertical blinds on the other side of the sliding glass door for her to get glimpses inside the main room. He'd left a lamp burning, enough to illuminate most of the area she could see.

"Anything?" Aaron asked in a low voice from behind her.

"It's tidy enough," she said, "but he hasn't cleared out. I see some of his things lying around. There are boxes stacked on the bar. Quite a few boxes. Different sizes, from about shoebox-size to, I don't know, microwave-size, maybe."

"Interesting."

"Should I go in and look?"

He was looking toward the road. "Not unless you want to tell your I-smelled-smoke story to Landon personally. He just parked in the driveway."

She hopped back from the door. "Oh. Uh—"

He held out his hand and smiled reassuringly. "Let's go back to my place. If anyone asks, we've just been out for a stroll."

Putting as much distance between themselves and the cabin as they could without actually running, they headed for his back door. When they were clear of Landon's cabin, they slowed their steps, moving closer to each other to continue the illusion that they were aware of nothing but each other.

"Hey! Who's there?"

Shelby didn't have to fake her startled jump. Placing her free hand on her pounding heart, she peered at Terrence Landon, who stood at the front corner of his cabin, glaring at them. Either he'd spotted movement as he'd driven up, or he'd simply been checking the perimeters of his cabin upon his return. She was satisfied that she and Aaron were far enough away from his porch that he wouldn't be able to be certain she'd been on it, but she still spoke breezily to reassure him.

"Mr. Landon, it's me, Shelby Bell. I hope we didn't startle you. Aaron and I have just been for a walk down by the water."

His skinny face was darkened by a suspicious scowl. "You weren't inside my cabin?"

"No, of course not. Why, do you need anything? I

can have housekeeping here first thing in the morning, if you—"

"No." He turned away. "I don't need anything."

"Okay, well, be sure and let us know if you do. Good night, Mr.—" But she was talking to air. He'd already hurried away.

She looked up at Aaron and whispered, "That guy is so—"

"—weird," he finished with her. "Yes, I know. But still not enough cause to call out the National Guard."

She walked with him through his back door. "I think I'm officially giving up the investigation of Terrence Landon. I was worried that he was doing something in there that would at the very least reflect badly on the resort, or cause us legal problems at the worst. After that debacle with Hannah's evil ex last year, I guess I was still just a little paranoid and overimaginative. Maybe he's as crooked as they come, in addition to being freaking bug-nuts, but as long as he gives me no further reason for concern, I'll leave him alone. I just hope he checks out Wednesday, as he implied he will. A nice young honeymoon couple would be more than welcome to take his place there."

Locking the door behind them, he closed the blinds. Tightly. "Does that mean I'm fired?"

She laughed. "You were never hired," she reminded him. "But you are hereby released from the favor I asked of you."

"Hmm. I was rather hoping I could rush in, guns blazing, to rescue you from the nefarious drug dealer in Cabin Seven," he said with such exaggerated regret that she had to laugh again.

"You nut," she said, resting her hands on his chest. "I never expected that from you."

He frowned. "You don't think I could have done it? Just because I'm not a P.I. like my brother—"

Though he was still teasing, she wanted to make something very clear. "Whatever skills Andrew may or may not have as a private investigator, he never had the same effect on me that you do," she murmured, lifting her head to nip a little kiss against his firm jaw. "If I was going to place myself in the hands of either of you, it would be you."

"I do like having you in my hands." As if to reinforce the comment, he slid his palms slowly up and down her sides, bringing them to rest on her hips to pull her closer to him. He lowered his mouth to hers and spoke against her lips, "Any other favors I can do for you now that Landon's out of the way?"

Wrapping her arms around his neck, she pressed herself against him. "I'm sure I can think of a few."

Some small, rational, distant part of her mind warned her somberly that she *was* going to be hurt. Footloose Aaron would soon tire of hanging shingles and mowing grass—would probably grow tired of her, as well—and he'd move on. Politely, she was sure. Sensitively. As considerately as possible, under the circumstances. He would probably give her that all-too-familiar speech about hoping they could always be friends. He cared about her, he would always respect and admire her, it wasn't her, it was him…yadda, yadda, yadda. The speech had hurt bad enough coming from Pete, and she hadn't even cared about him all that much. It was going to break her heart when she heard it from Aaron, with whom she had tumbled head over heels in love.

She could walk away now. Pull her lips from beneath him, drag herself out of his arms, put a safe, sensible distance between them. Yet her heart would still be broken when he left—and she wouldn't even have these sweet memories to comfort her.

Drawing her lips from his, she smiled mistily. "Let's go upstairs, Aaron."

She didn't have to ask him twice.

Aaron watched Shelby dress later with an expression that felt uncomfortably like a pout. "I always hate to see you leave," he said, though she probably already knew that, considering how many ways he had tried to detain her.

Brushing her hair out of her eyes, she smiled at him. "I really need to go. There's always a nondenominational sunrise service in the pavilion at 7:00 a.m. We don't charge admission to the resort before noon on Sundays, so occasionally people from the surrounding towns attend the services in addition to interested guests. I'm usually there to make sure there aren't any problems, then I take the rest of Sunday off unless I'm filling in for someone."

He glanced at the clock. "You aren't going to get much sleep."

Shrugging, she said, "That's okay. I don't need much."

"Did you ride your bike over?"

"No, I walked tonight."

He looked around for his shoes. "I'll drive you back."

"Seriously?" She laughed. "You will not. It's a ten-minute walk across a resort filled with people."

"People who are asleep," he pointed out.

"And who will wake up if I should scream or shout. Really, Aaron, I do this all the time."

His left eyebrow shot up. "Leave one of the cabins in the middle of the night?"

"Not like this," she chided with a shake of her head. "But I've been called out for problems in the middle of the night, just as the rest of the family has. And I've never felt unsafe here. It's home."

She couldn't read his expression when he shrugged and conceded. "Your choice, of course."

Patting his cheek, she said, "Don't worry, Aaron, I'll be fine. I'll see you tomorrow."

She kissed him, then headed for the door. "Meet me at the pavilion in the morning if you're interested and awake that early. It's always a lovely service."

"Maybe I will. Sounds nice."

"We could have breakfast afterward, before you join Uncle Bryan on the roof again."

"You're on."

"I'll count the minutes," she promised him, and though she spoke jokingly, she meant every word.

"So will I," he said, and he sounded entirely serious—which probably meant he was joking, she thought with a laugh at herself as she stepped out his door.

They were quite an odd couple, temporary though it might be. She wondered if she would ever think of him in the future without wistfully wondering what might have been.

There was only one totally dark stretch between Aaron's cabin and her mobile home, just after stepping off the main road past the private-drive sign. It was perhaps ten yards of deep shadows from which she could see the houses ahead, but was probably invisible to anyone looking back at her from there. She never thought twice about that dark stretch, no matter what hour she walked, drove or biked it. As she'd told Aaron, this was home.

Something slammed into the back of her head. She stumbled forward, the lights ahead of her splintering, blurring into darkness. As if from a distance, she felt her chin make contact with the pavement. And then felt nothing at all.

Chapter Ten

Aaron lay on his back in the rumpled bed, suddenly feeling all the aches of the day. His body craved rest, but he was having trouble shutting down his mind. He wished he could pass what remained of the night with Shelby wrapped in his arms, only to make love again with the rising of the sun.

He'd spent a lot of time with her in the past few days. More hours, perhaps, than he'd spent with Elaina during an entire week while they'd seen each other. Granted, he and Elaina had both been busy with jobs and other activities, but he realized now that as hot as the sex had been between them, as often as he'd wanted to come back for more, he'd had no overwhelming desire to spend time with Elaina outside the bedroom. They'd had few interests in common—or so he'd learned when she'd stopped pretending to find everything he said utterly fascinating—and when they weren't in bed, they'd struggled to find something else to do that entertained them both. She'd loved fancy parties, elegant dining, shopping, cruises. He'd rather be on a mountain trail, in a boat, on a bike or watching a game, none of which she'd enjoyed. He couldn't imagine her skimming over the water straddling a personal watercraft, no makeup, hair in the wind, sun on her face. Just remembering how Shelby had looked exactly that way made his whole body harden.

He was getting in too deep with her. He shouldn't be this preoccupied with her after such a short time. Definitely he shouldn't have been so teeth-grindingly jealous when she'd driven off with ol' Pete earlier. For all he knew, she could get back with Pete again after Aaron went back to Dallas, despite her assurances that it wasn't going to happen. The thought of her kissing that other man, letting him touch her… He found himself grinding his teeth again, and had to make a conscious effort to relax his jaw.

Flopping over on the bed, he closed his eyes and tried to will himself to sleep. He was just tired. Hard to think clearly in this state of exhaustion, he assured himself. The rest of his life was so unsettled, maybe that was affecting his judgment about Shelby, too. He didn't have to say goodbye to her forever just because he had to go pursue a new career path. They could stay in touch, see each other occasionally, maybe. The resort wasn't all that far from Dallas. Or maybe he could find something closer. Yes, she came with a lot of family entanglements, something he'd carefully avoided with other women, because he had enough of that already in his life. But he liked Shelby's family—even her grandfather, who seemed to be convinced he wasn't who he said he was. And her parents, who'd given him the evil eye at lunch today for encouraging Steven and not discouraging Lori.

Maybe someday when he'd gotten his own life in order, when he was settled into a career he found challenging and fulfilling, when he was ready to take on the complications of someone else's needs and obligations, when he felt as though he had something worthwhile to offer in return—maybe then he'd see if Shelby was interested in pursuing something more than a vacation hookup with him. If by then she hadn't already found someone who could offer those things before Aaron got around to it.

Groaning, he pulled the sheet over his head and started mentally counting by sevens, usually a sure-fire way to lull himself to sleep. It took him a bit longer than usual that night.

He was jolted out of a sound sleep before sunrise by a sharp knock on his door. It took him a couple of groggy minutes to realize what he'd heard, but a follow-up pounding brought him to his feet. Tugging on a pair of jeans, he glanced at the clock, noted that it wasn't even yet 6:00 a.m., then headed barefoot down the stairs, dragging a white T-shirt over his head on the way. He opened the door, then blinked in surprise upon finding Maggie on his porch.

"Maggie? What's wrong? Has something happened?"

Her expression looked strained in the watery security lighting, her face pale in contrast with her dark brown hair. "Please tell me Shelby's here with you. If she is, I'm sorry I woke you, but I just needed to—"

"Shelby's not here, Maggie," he cut in with a frown. "She left a few hours ago to go back to her trailer. Why?"

Maggie's hand wasn't steady when she showed him

the cell phone in her hand. "It's Shelby's. I woke up early and wanted coffee, but I was out. I didn't want to wake anyone else, so I decided to run over to the marina and get a pot started there. Uncle Bryan always has coffee going by six-thirty for the early fishermen, so I figured it wouldn't hurt to make it early…"

She was babbling, her voice high-pitched and nervous. "Maggie," he cut in quickly, impatiently. "What about Shelby?"

She drew a quick breath. "The golf cart headlights reflected off something on the road by the private drive sign, so I stopped to see what it was. It was this, Shelby's phone. Finding it there made me nervous, so I had to go check on her. I mean, I figured she just dropped it or something and maybe didn't know she'd lost it or couldn't find it in the darkness or—"

Taking another steadying breath, she finished, "I went to her house, let myself in with the emergency key we all carry, and I saw that her bed was still made. I know she's been spending a lot of time with you, and I figured maybe—well, maybe she spent the night. But something still just didn't feel right, so I had to check, even if it embarrassed all of us."

"She's not here," Aaron repeated numbly, going cold inside as he remembered his last glimpse of Shelby walking jauntily away from his cabin, smiling and unafraid. "Could she be with her parents? Her brother or sister?"

"I don't know why she would be, but now that I know she's not here, I'm going to call them," Maggie said grimly.

"Call them." Aaron tugged her inside, then turned for the stairs. "I'll get some shoes."

It took him two minutes to throw on shoes and pull

a polo shirt over his tee. Maggie was still talking on the phone when he bolted back downstairs, but he could tell she wasn't getting good news.

"They don't know where she is," she whispered to Aaron, as though her throat was too tight to allow her full voice to push through. "Lori didn't come home last night, but she'd already told them she was staying with friends. Shelby's car is still at her trailer and she didn't leave any messages for anyone. I'm really scared, Aaron. Why was her phone on the road?"

He had his own phone in his hand. His first instinct was to call his brother—the one person he always turned to in times of trouble, no matter what issues they might be dealing with personally. His second thought was to call the police. He forced himself to hold off on both until he knew what to tell them.

"You haven't been to the marina yet, have you?" he confirmed with Maggie.

She shook her head. "I came straight here. Uncle C.J. said he was headed that way. Everyone's going to spread out and look for her."

"She told me there's a church service this morning. That she usually goes to sort of monitor things. Could she be at the pavilion already?" She could have just dropped the phone, he reminded himself. Probably hadn't noticed. Maybe she'd had the same idea as Maggie about the marina coffee.

Maggie bit her lip. "I can't imagine why. No one would be there this early."

"Let's go find out."

Instinct made him look toward Terrence Landon's cabin on his way to the golf cart. As usual, the blinds were tightly closed. He thought he saw a very faint glow of light from inside, but it was probably just a dimmed lamp serving as a night-light. He had no reason to believe Landon had anything to do with Shelby going missing. For one thing, he'd watched her head off in the other direction when she'd left him.

Which didn't mean he wouldn't be pounding on Landon's door if Shelby didn't turn up soon.

"What the hell have you done, Russ?"

Shuddering at the barely repressed fury in the gravelly male voice, Shelby shrank back against the wall in Cabin Seven. Her head pounded. Tied behind her, her arms ached. Her ankles were bound so tightly that she couldn't feel her feet, but she had a feeling they were going to hurt like the devil if—when she was released, she amended quickly, trying to stay as positive as she could considering the circumstances.

It was dark in the cabin and her vision was still blurry from the hit on the head, but she could just see the two men standing on the far side of the room, glaring back at her. One was Terrence Landon—or Russ, as the other man had just called him. The angry newcomer was a man she'd seen once before, the pudgy middle-aged guy who'd visited earlier in the week.

"She's been snooping around the whole time I've been here, Lowell," Landon countered defensively. "I think she might have been in the cabin earlier today. She'd have seen the stuff."

"You mean the stuff I told you not to leave lying around?"

Landon growled. "How was I supposed to know she'd come in?"

Shelby wanted to tell him that she hadn't set foot inside the cabin, but because he'd stuck duct tape over her mouth, all she could do was mumble irritably.

"Shut up," Landon snapped at her before turning back to the other man. "All I was waiting for was for you to get here with the cash. I'll help you load your car with your stuff, then we can clear out of here, probably before anyone knows she's missing. I'll carry her out to my car under a blanket, hang on to her until I know we've gotten away clear, then I'll let her go or something."

Shelby didn't like the sound of that "or something."

She'd known from the start that the so-called Terrence Landon was strange, but she'd figured out in the past hours that the guy wasn't particularly bright, either. He was such a bumbling TV stereotype of a bad guy that she might have laughed had she not woken up trussed up like a turkey and with him pacing and sweating, neither an encouraging indication of his stability. Lowell had shown up about ten minutes ago.

She couldn't see a clock, but she thought it was probably somewhere between six-thirty and seven, judging from the light filtering in through the blinds and the sound of the awakening resort outside. It had been almost 2:00 a.m. when Landon had followed her and grabbed her on her way home. She didn't know how he'd gotten her back to the cabin without anyone seeing him, but maybe it hadn't been all that hard. As Aaron had pointed out when she'd left him, not many campers were awake at that hour. She hadn't had a chance to scream and awaken anyone. By the time she'd come to, hurting and disoriented, she'd already been tied up. Landon had tried interrogating her about what she knew, but he hadn't believed her repeated vows that she didn't know anything. He'd taped her mouth when she'd tried to warn him that he was making a huge mistake holding her hostage.

People would be gathering at the pavilion soon. Aaron would be there, she reminded herself hopefully. Would he know to question Landon when she didn't show up? How long would it take him to look for her, to figure out that she hadn't just overslept? By that time Landon and Lowell could have left the resort, taking her with them.

"What you do with her is up to you," Lowell growled. "I want nothing to do with it. You've got five minutes to help me get my stuff out of here. I'm not paying you a cent until it's in my car and I know I'm going to drive away without any trouble."

Landon nodded curtly. "Keep a watch out for the guy next door. I think he might be a cop. He's been watching me, too. That's why I called you and told you I had to get out of here today. I didn't know it would take you almost four freaking hours to get here. If I'd know you were way the hell on the other side of Dallas when I called, I'd have already cleared out and met you somewhere else."

"A cop?" Lowell's already-ruddy face reddened even more. "That guy who was staring at me the other day is a cop?"

Grunting, Shelby shook her head fervently, though she wasn't sure they even noticed.

"Look, I don't know that for sure." Landon sounded even more nervous now. "Could be she just has a nosy boyfriend. But I'm hanging on to her for insurance, just to make sure no one tries to stop us from leaving if they want her back safe."

Lowell already had an armful of boxes and was headed for the door. "You don't have enough sense to pour piss out of a boot, Russ. Don't know why I was stupid enough to get hooked up with you, but I am not going down with you for kidnapping. This is all on you."

Landon grabbed several more boxes and followed him, shooting a hard look at Shelby. "If you'd just minded your own business…"

She wished sincerely now that she had.

It took less than ten minutes for the men to carry out all the boxes. "That's it?" Lowell looked around with narrowed eyes, clutching a fat briefcase in one hand. "That's all of it?"

Landon nodded. "I'll call you when I've found another place to stay and have some more stuff for you."

Shoving the case at him, Lowell muttered, "You said this place would be good for the summer. Said no one paid attention to just another summer camper. Said folks mind their own business at a fishing resort."

"Most of them do," Landon grumbled, turning another scowl toward Shelby.

Lowell turned toward the door. "I'm out of here."

"Wait. I could use your help getting her out to the car."

"I told you you're on your own with that. It's your own stupidity for grabbing her in the first place."

"I had to know what she's seen. Who she told. She said she hasn't seen anything or told anyone, but I don't believe her. I had to have some insurance that I'd get away from here safe."

Shaking his head and muttering, Lowell reached for the doorknob, only to freeze when someone knocked. Lowell and Landon stared at each other for a moment, and then Landon called out nervously, "Who is it?"

"Mr. Landon, it's Maggie Bell. I'm sorry to bother you at this hour, but I need to ask you something."

"You'll have to come back later."

"Please, sir, just a quick question."

"Get rid of them," Lowell hissed.

"Give me a minute," Landon called out. Moving with clumsy haste, he threw the briefcase into a cabinet, then reached for Shelby. She shrank back from him, but he had his sweaty hands on her forearms before she could evade him. He threw her over his shoulder and carried her to the small storage closet under the stairs that led up to the sleeping loft. Shoving her unceremoniously inside with the broom and the vacuum cleaner, he stood back.

"Not a sound from you," he grated, pointing an unsteady finger at her. "I'm warning you."

He slammed the door, leaving her in dusty-scented darkness. She leaned against the hollow-core door, straining to hear through the thin wood, ignoring the pain in her shoulder where something dug into her skin through her blouse.

"Get upstairs. If anyone sees you, you're a business associate, here for a meeting," she heard Landon say to Lowell.

She heard footsteps on the stairs, and then the front door opened. "What do you want?"

"We're looking for my cousin," Maggie said, her voice slightly muffled by the closet door. "Shelby. She's gone missing."

"I'm sorry to hear that, but what makes you think I'd know where she is?" Landon demanded.

Shelby's heart clenched when she heard Aaron's deep voice. "She left my place at almost two this morning. We were hoping maybe you saw something."

"At two in the morning? I was asleep. Even had I been awake, I don't make a habit of spying on my neighbors, unlike some people."

"Maybe you heard something?" Maggie asked, her voice sounding so strained as to be almost unrecognizable. "Needless to say, we're afraid something has happened to her."

"Sorry, but I can't help you." The response was brusque, and sounded as though he was moving to close the door.

Shelby was sure Maggie and Aaron were doing everything they could to look beyond Landon, who was undoubtedly blocking the doorway. She tried to cry out, but the only sounds that emerged from her were stifled grunts. In desperation, she threw herself against the door, against the cleaning supplies around her, resulting in a satisfactory crash.

"What was that?" Aaron asked sharply, raising her hopes.

"That was none of your business," Landon snapped.

"Mr. Landon—"

"I'm afraid I'm the one who made that racket." Shelby groaned hoarsely when she heard Lowell descend the stairs, speaking with rueful humor. "I just dropped an armful of grooming supplies upstairs. You'll have to forgive my, um, friend for his rudeness."

"Mr. Landon, if we could just—"

"Good luck finding your cousin," Landon said quickly. "I'll let you know if I see anything."

He slammed the door, probably in their faces. Shelby whimpered.

Lowell waited only a couple of minutes before saying to Landon, "That's all the help I'm giving you. They catch you with her now, you're on your own."

"Lowell, wait—"

The door slammed and Shelby heard Landon cursing steadily, pacing and slamming his fist on any solid

surface. He was angry, scared, trapped by his own stupidity—none of which boded well for her. She was still
leaning against the door when he jerked it open and she
fell out of the storage closet, landing in an ignoble heap
at his feet. For a moment she thought he might kick her,
and she drew as far away as she could.

He reached down and hauled her upright. With her
feet tied together, she hopped awkwardly, trying to find
her balance. He hit her across the face with the back of
one hand, almost knocking her down again. Pain ex-
ploding in her cheek, she would have fallen had he not
roughly caught her. "I told you to stay quiet."

She glared at him over the tape, trying to express
with her eyes all the contemptuous thoughts going
through her mind. He looked as though he wanted to
hit her again, but instead, he pushed her toward the
kitchen. Retrieving the briefcase, he threw the shoulder strap over his arm, then drew a steak knife from a
drawer. She eyed it nervously, knowing the blade wasn't
extremely sharp, but also aware that it could do plenty
of damage as it was. Leaning over, he slashed the tape
around her ankles, freeing her feet. Before she could
even take a step, he had the knife at her throat. With
her arms still bound behind her back, there was little
she could do to ward him off.

"We're going to walk out to my car," he said, his face
shiny now with perspiration. "We're driving out of this
place. If we make it out without interference, I'll let you
go after we've put some distance behind us. If anyone
tries to stop us…"

He pushed the blade a bit closer to her throat, letting
that gesture finish the warning for him.

She didn't see how this could end well. Landon or
Russ or whatever his name was, was losing control,

becoming more irrational by the moment. Her family was looking for her and she couldn't see them standing back and letting him drive away with her. Not to mention what Aaron might do. Someone was going to be hurt. And she was the one closest to the sharp edge of the blade.

Staying close behind her, he moved her to the door, where he fumbled with the doorknob while keeping the knife close to her throat. A dozen different schemes raced through her mind. She could try to break away and run. She could deliberately fall, buying herself some time while he hauled her back up to her feet. She could try head-butting or kicking him.

In all of those mental scenarios, she ended up with a nasty slice or stab wound.

"Don't waste time. Straight to the car. You're driving." He pushed her ahead of him out the door, using her as a shield in front of him.

He hadn't accounted for an attack from behind. Though she couldn't see exactly what happened, Shelby sensed the hit to the back of Landon's head. He grunted and stumbled forward, his knife-wielding arm jerking outward. Someone caught that arm and swung Landon away from her. Someone else grabbed her and tugged her backward. Reacting instinctively, she started to resist.

"Shelby, it's me. Maggie."

The sound of her cousin's voice in her ear made her go limp with relief. Hearing the thud of a fist, a cry of pain, she stumbled around to look. Landon was on the ground, struggling but obviously overpowered. Aaron straddled him, a lethal look in his eyes as he drove a fist into Landon's face. Shelby heard shouts, running feet. Her father and uncle and some other men she didn't immediately identify appeared, surrounding Aaron and Landon, pulling them apart. Someone shouted instructions to call the police. Landon resisted another few minutes, then sagged in defeat as several men restrained him.

Abandoning Landon, Aaron rushed to Shelby. Maggie had been fumbling with the bindings on her wrists. "Let me," Aaron said, his voice husky.

His eyes locked with hers. She thought he looked a little pale, but maybe that was because she was seeing him through a sudden film of tears. Very gently, he peeled the tape from her face. The adhesive tugged at her irritated skin, pulled at her dry, cracked lips, but she was so very glad to have it gone that she hardly noticed. She tried to speak, but her voice came out a hoarse croak.

"Are you all right? Did he hurt you?"

"I'm okay," she whispered.

"I'll get you some water," Maggie said, turning to dash into the cabin.

"Shelby. Baby, are you okay?" Her dad stood close by while Aaron released her wrists. She moaned in equal parts pain and relief when the bindings fell away and her arms dropped to her side.

Aaron kept an arm around her waist to support her while her dad hovered around her, rubbing her arm, stroking her hair, struggling to maintain his usual composure. Her uncle patted her back. Maggie returned with the water, then fluttered around while her dad held the glass to her parched lips. Pushing the glass away, Shelby looked up at Aaron, giving him a full view of her face.

His stormy eyes narrowed to slits. He lifted a hand to brush the very tips of his fingers against her cheek.

He didn't hurt her, but she felt the tenderness of the area he touched, and realized belatedly that it must be bruised from where Landon had hit her.

Grinding his teeth, Aaron started to turn away, murder in his eyes as he surged toward the man still being restrained by volunteers. Shelby reached out just in time to catch his arm. "No," she rasped. "Don't."

Aaron stood very still for a few moments, almost quivering with a need to avenge her. "Please," she whispered, not wanting to let him out of touching distance.

Sighing in resignation, he contented himself with one last irate look toward Landon, then he turned his back to the man and drew Shelby into his arms, heedless of the gathering crowd of onlookers. Both her father and uncle were talking into phones; she assumed they were notifying everyone that she had been found. The sound of sirens was growing closer. She braced herself for police interviews.

"The other man. His name was Lowell," she whispered, her throat still too dry and tight for her voice to sound normal.

"I reported his license number and a description of his car and told them he was a participant in a kidnapping," Aaron informed her. "He won't get far."

She nodded and rested her cheek on his shoulder. Her head was beginning to spin. She was operating on no sleep, still quivering with residual shock. "I think I need to sit down."

Her father moved toward the door. "Let's go inside."

She stiffened. "Not in there."

She would go inside Cabin Seven again, of course. She wouldn't let Landon's actions make her permanently afraid in this place that had always been part of her home. But she wasn't ready quite yet.

"I've called an ambulance," Maggie said.

"I don't need an ambulance!"

"Shelby, there's blood on the back of your head, your hands are so swollen you can hardly move your fingers, there's no color in your face and your eyes look funny. We'll let the EMTs decide whether you need to be transported," Maggie said flatly, the strain of the ordeal showing in the lines around her firm mouth.

"We'll go to my cabin to wait," Aaron offered. "I'll carry you."

"No." Drawing on every ounce of remaining strength, she straightened away from him, her chin high. "I'll walk."

Aaron nodded and took her hand. "We'll all go together."

Followed closely by her father, uncle and cousin, and knowing that the rest of the family would surely arrive soon, Shelby limped at Aaron's side toward his cabin.

Two hours later, Aaron sat in a chair in a hospital room, watching Shelby as she slept. There was no need to sit guard now, of course. Terrence Landon—or Russell King, as Andrew had discovered, calling after all the excitement was over to report his findings—had been hauled away. He was being charged with assault, kidnapping, fencing stolen goods and probably a few other crimes thrown in for good measure. Charles Lowell was also in custody, having been detained with a trunkful of stolen jewelry, silver and other items of value. More arrests were pending.

For some reason those wannabe criminal geniuses had decided that a busy fishing resort was an ideal, anonymous place for a temporary fencing operation after they'd been forced to leave Austin when authorities had gotten too close to catching them. In another few days, they'd have moved on to another equally random location. Had Shelby not sensed that something was wrong and been so determined to protect the reputation of her family's once-bitten business, they might actually have pulled it off this time. As Landon had hoped, everyone else had been too preoccupied with either running the resort or enjoying it to pay much attention to the odd occupant of Cabin Seven.

Aaron wasn't the only one in the room with Shelby now. Her parents and sister sat on the other side of the bed, talking in low voices as Sarah filled in Lori, who had arrived only a short while before, on the morning's events. The tension between Lori and her parents had been set aside for now as they'd come together in support of Shelby. Steven was at home seething with frustration that his injuries had prevented him from participating in the search for Shelby. He was probably even more determined now to recuperate fully and train for a career that would allow him to be an active first responder.

Shelby's grandparents, aunt and uncle had all gathered in Aaron's cabin to wait with the rest of them for the ambulance to arrive, and to support her as she'd talked to the police. They had hovered around Shelby until she'd looked close to snapping. Aaron understood how scared they'd all been, and how relieved they were that she had been relatively unharmed. He knew both feelings all too well.

Her grandparents, especially, had been very vocal about their emotions.

"I can't handle much more of this," Mimi had announced, furiously fanning her face with one hand. "Between Steven getting hurt and then giving his notice and Hannah in trouble and now criminals staying in our own cabin, kidnapping our granddaughter from right under our noses—what is the world coming to?"

"It's okay, Mimi," Maggie said soothingly, one hand on her grandmother's shoulder. "Shelby's going to be fine. Aaron rescued her."

"Hmm. You're sure you're not Andrew?" Pop had demanded, peering hard at Aaron. "The way you handled that situation looked a lot like a professional P.I.—like the man who already rescued this family once before."

Aaron had chuckled shortly, as had several of the others, enjoying the lighter moment in the otherwise grim morning. "I'm still Aaron, Pop."

"Humph. Well, I guess you've got more in common with your brother than a nice face," the older man had conceded, slapping Aaron on the shoulder hard enough almost to make him stagger forward.

Shelby and her parents had convinced everyone else to stay behind and take care of the resort when the EMTs had determined that she should probably be scanned for concussion. No one had attempted to convince Aaron to stay behind, not that they would have succeeded if they'd tried.

"I'll help you finish the roof later," he'd said to Bryan on his way out. "I just have to know Shelby's okay first."

Bryan had nodded in understanding. "The roof can wait. Take care of my niece. I'll need to run the marina until C.J. gets back, anyway."

Shelby had a mild concussion and a sprained wrist, but other than needing three stitches at the back of her head, a stretch bandage on her left wrist, fluids and rest, she required no further treatment. She would be free to leave in an hour or so, after she'd received a full IV bag of fluids.

"I still don't know how you figured out she was in that cabin," C.J. said in a low voice, leaving his wife and younger daughter talking on the other side of the room as he joined Aaron.

Aaron shrugged. "When we couldn't find her anywhere else, that was the first possibility that occurred to me. Finding her phone on the road implied to me that she'd been startled, taken against her will. Though there were other possibilities, I kept thinking of the tension between her and Landon—er, the guy that called himself Landon. I wanted to get a look at his face when we canvassed the resort. I knew the minute I saw him that he was hiding something. When I heard the crash from the storage closet, I was even more convinced, though his accomplice tried to explain away the noise by saying he'd caused it."

"But you didn't try to rush inside then?"

"I needed a chance to form a plan," Aaron admitted. "Maggie kept watch while I went around to the back and looked in through a crack in the blinds Shelby and I had discovered last night. I saw Lowell leave, then watched Landon pull Shelby out of the closet."

He had also seen the knife in the man's hand. His first enraged instinct had been to crash through the glass door, maybe slamming into it with a patio chair. But then he'd thought of the delay that could be caused by tangling with the broken glass and blinds—long enough for Landon to use that knife in panic—and he'd forced himself to stay in control. With his limited viewpoint, he hadn't seen Landon hit Shelby, which was just as well, as he'd have probably lost all objectivity at that point, but he'd been able to time his arrival around the front of the cabin in time to attack from behind. His heart had been in his throat, his stomach in knots as he'd prayed he would be fast enough to keep Shelby from being harmed. Determination—and the years of martial arts training he'd taken with his brother—had paid off. The element of surprise had been in his favor, as had Landon's frantic ineptitude. But he never wanted to be placed in a situation like that again.

"You saved her life," C.J. said, his voice gruff with emotion. "I don't know how to thank you."

Aaron was aware that Shelby's life might not have been in danger in the first place if she hadn't dallied in his bed for so many hours, if she hadn't walked alone in the darkest part of the night. It still made him physically ill to think of the hours she had spent in pain and terror only a few yards away from where he'd slept in his comfortable bed.

He should have seen her safely home, he berated himself, for far from the first time. Despite her protests, despite her familiarity with the resort and her confidence that she would be fine, he should have insisted, even at the risk of bruising her pride. Not because she was incapable of caring for herself, but because they'd both had reason to suspect something shady was going on with Terrence Landon/Russell King and should have taken reasonable precautions. It was going to be a long time, if ever, before he got past that guilt.

She shifted in the bed and opened her eyes, drawing all attention to her. She smiled weakly at her mother, then turned her head to seek out Aaron. "You're still here."

"I'm still here."

"I'm getting a little fuzzy on the details, but I can't remember if I ever thanked you." Though sleepy, her voice sounded stronger now, more like herself.

"Not necessary," he assured her.

Still smiling, she allowed her heavy eyelids to drift downward again. "Nevertheless…"

Feeling her family's eyes turning to him, Aaron cleared his throat. "Now that we know Shelby's going to be okay, I should really get back to that roof. It really should be finished before the rain that's being predicted for later this week."

"Maybe you could give me a lift," C.J. said. "I'll spell Bryan at the marina so he can finish the roofing job with you. Sarah, you and Lori can get Shelby home, can't you? You'll call us if you need help?"

"Of course," Sarah said, moving to lay a hand protectively on Shelby's arm.

"We can take care of her," Lori agreed, tossing a strand of black hair out of her eyes.

C.J. bent over the bed to kiss his daughter's forehead. "You do what the doctors tell you, you hear?"

Without opening her eyes, she smiled. "Yes, Daddy."

"I'll see you at home."

"'Kay."

Aaron took C.J.'s place, resting a hand gently on Shelby's bandaged wrist. "If you need anything, have someone call me. I'll be here."

She opened her eyes then, her smile softening. "I know. You Walker boys are quite the heroes to this family."

Something about that comment bothered him, but he decided he would mull it over later. After a momentary hesitation, he bent to brush his lips across hers. It wasn't as if her family didn't know she'd spent most of the night with him, after all.

"See you, Shelby."

Sighing lightly, she let her lids fall. "See you."

He paused another moment, his gaze locked on the bruise on her face, then he turned to C.J. "Ready?"

Chapter Eleven

Because of the late start, it was late afternoon by the time Aaron and Bryan finished the roofing job on the little cabin. The family had gathered again at the home of Shelby's parents that evening, earlier than they could usually get together because the marina, store and grill closed early on Sundays. Dinner tonight was Texas chili and jalapeño corn bread prepared by Mimi and Maggie, something they'd been able to throw together fairly easily and stretch to feed a crowd.

Aaron joined them for the meal, but Shelby noticed he was rather quiet—not that he had much chance to get a word in. Still rattled by the events of the day, her family was even more verbal and energetic than usual, everyone talking at once, all of them chagrined that Shelby had tried to warn them about Terrence Landon and they'd all brushed off her concerns.

"We really are going to learn to take you seriously

from now on when you start spouting your improbable theories," Steven told her, his smile lopsided. He'd been more attentive to Shelby than usual that evening, no doubt still perturbed that he hadn't been there for her earlier. They'd teasingly compared concussions and other injuries, but Shelby had been aware that Steven was as relieved that she had survived her ordeal as she was that she still had her brother. They could argue, compete or tease, but through it all they were family—and they loved each other.

She held up her hands in a gesture of surrender, the left still swaddled in a stretch bandage. "No more conspiracies for me," she vowed. "From now on, I'm keeping my head down and focusing on my numbers and spreadsheets."

"That would be a shame," her father said unexpectedly. "Had you made a habit of that, we might never have known that Wade had been siphoning money from us. And who knows, Terrence Landon or Russell King or whatever the hell his name is might have decided this was a good place to return to whenever he needed a convenient retreat from which to run his fencing operation for a few weeks at a time. You did good, honey."

She flushed a little in pleasure. As much as she loved him, her father wasn't one to indulge in complimentary speeches. He was also the one who'd been most impatient with some of her more fanciful schemes and imaginings, and with reason at times. "Well, maybe I'll try to restrain myself to only crying wolf when I actually see one," she said.

He looked as though he tried to smile back at her but just couldn't. "You certainly saw one this time."

After dinner and dessert, Shelby announced that she was exhausted. Though she'd rested most of the

day after her ordeal, she was still bone-weary, probably more from lingering trauma than lack of sleep.
Her head hurt some, but not so badly that she wanted
to accept her mother's offer to stay there rather than return to her own place. She wanted to sleep in her own
home—preferably not alone, she thought, glancing at
Aaron from beneath her lashes, but better by herself in
her own bed than being hovered over any longer in her
parents' house.

"I'll see you home," Aaron said, rising to his feet
when she did.

She'd hoped he would offer.

After saying good-night to everyone, promising them
all that her doors would be securely locked despite the
threat being over and assuring them that she would
see them tomorrow, she was finally able to step outside with Aaron.

They took a golf cart to her place, with Aaron behind the wheel. It wasn't a long walk, but still more
than Shelby felt up to just then. He accompanied her
inside, glancing around curiously, which made her realize it was actually the first time he'd been in her trailer.
The home had come furnished in neutral colors, but
she'd added touches of bright accents to reflect her own
tastes. She'd left it fairly tidy, though an open book, an
empty diet soda can and a candy bar wrapper sat on the
coffee table. Evidence of a snack attack while reading,
she thought with a tired smile.

"Can I get you anything?" she asked Aaron, moving
toward the couch.

He had paused just inside the door. "No, thanks. Unless you need me for anything else, I'm going to clear
out and let you get some rest."

"Oh." Disappointment flooded through her as she turned back toward him. "You're leaving now?"

Hands in his jeans pockets, he nodded. "Unless you need me to stay."

"I don't need you to stay," she said quietly. "But I'd like for you to."

She wondered if he understood that she wasn't talking only about tonight.

He couldn't seem to quite meet her eyes. "You need sleep. The docs said there's no reason for you to be monitored or anything during the night, right?"

Swallowing hard, she replied, "They said I'll be fine."

"Are you in any pain?"

"Just a mild headache and my wrist is sore, but I think an over-the-counter pain reliever will be enough. I don't like taking the prescription stuff."

He nodded, still looking oddly uncomfortable. "So, you have everything you need? You got your phone back, right?"

"Yes, it's in my pocket. Fully charged and working. Maggie took care of that for me."

"Feel free to call or text if you need me."

"Aaron," she said when he started to turn. "What's going on?"

Staring at the doorknob, he said, "I know you're tired. You need to rest."

"Why won't you look at me?"

He glanced over his shoulder. "Because every time I see that bruise on your face, it makes me ache," he admitted.

"Aaron—"

His hand gripped the doorknob hard enough to whiten his knuckles. "I'm no hero, Shelby," he said roughly. "I'm not a private investigator like my brother or a firefighter like yours wants to be. I was the wrong person to ask to help you with Landon. I didn't take you seriously enough, and then when I did look into him, I made him so suspicious he grabbed you as insurance."

"That was not your fault. There was no way you could have predicted the man would completely lose his mind. And don't say you should have walked me home," she added quickly, predicting what he would probably say next. "You tried to insist and I wouldn't let you. That was entirely my decision."

He sighed and squeezed the back of his neck with one hand. "When Maggie came to me and told me you were missing, I nearly lost it."

"She said you were amazingly calm and collected. She told me she could tell you were worried, but you immediately started organizing a search and then told her you suspected Landon."

"I—"

"Aaron," she cut in firmly. "You figured out where I was and you took care of Landon without getting me hurt. You reported Lowell in time for the local police to stop him. I'm not going to embarrass you by calling you a hero, but I'm very glad you were on my side today."

"Every time I think that you were right next door for hours without me knowing, tied up and—"

"And absolutely certain that you would find me," she assured him, moving toward him to place a hand on his cheek. He had been so strong all day, and despite his denials, so heroic. She couldn't blame him for falling apart a little now.

He covered her hand with his own, then turned his

face to place a kiss in her palm. "I'm sorry for what you went through," he murmured.

"I was scared," she admitted softly. "And furious. But mostly I kept thinking of you, sending you mental signals where I was. Maybe you picked them up."

She was pleased to see his lips twitch with a hint of his smile, even though it didn't last very long. "Maybe I did."

"Don't go, Aaron."

His expression was conflicted. "I think it's better if I do tonight. And tomorrow—well, maybe it's time for you to thank me politely for the rescue and then send me on my way. I'll be suitably crushed and your ego will be bolstered, just like you planned."

"It was a stupid plan," she grumbled, rather mortified by his recounting of it.

He chuckled without much humor. "We'll play it however you want," he assured her. "But I still have to go. I've got a future to figure out."

A future she didn't fit into, he might as well have said. She stepped back and bit her lip. She really couldn't bear it if he gave her the speech about what a great pal he considered her to be.

"I guess I am tired," she said. "Thanks for seeing me home."

He nodded. "Call if you need me."

"I have my family nearby," she reminded him. The people who really cared about her, she added to herself.

He might have flinched a little, but then he nodded. "Do you want me to send one of them to you? Your mom? Maggie?"

"No. I don't need anyone. I'm fine." She was quite sure one of her family would have insisted on staying with her tonight had they not thought Aaron would be there instead. Which didn't mean any of them, with the possible exception of the younger generation, approved of her staying the night with a man she'd known such a short time. But they'd all agreed long ago that if they were going to work and live this closely, there had to be boundaries. Lori still got the parental-supervision treatment, mostly because she was still in school and they didn't approve of the guy she was seeing, but for the most part, they let Shelby make her own choices.

She didn't need her hand held to keep away the bad memories tonight. That wasn't why she wanted Aaron to stay.

"You're sure?"

"I'm sure. If I change my mind, I'll call someone."

"Good night, Shelby."

"Good night," she whispered.

Without looking back, he closed the door behind him.

Shelby sank slowly to the couch. She'd thought he would stay, she realized dazedly. Maybe not forever, but at least for tonight. As traumatic as the experience had been for both of them, she'd thought they could spend tonight wrapped in each other's arms, giving and seeking reassurance. Instead, he'd walked out without even looking at her.

Leaning back against the cushions, she tried to be angry with him. But something about the expression she'd seen on his face before he'd left had twisted her heart. After all that had happened to her in the past eighteen hours, she should be curled in a fetal position, whimpering. Instead, she was sitting here worrying about Aaron, wondering why his eyes had been so damned bleak.

A clipped laugh escaped her. She'd done it again, she thought with a shake of her head. Gotten in over her head. And she wasn't thinking about the bad man in Cabin Seven now.

Leaving the golf cart parked in front of Shelby's mobile home, Aaron headed grimly down the road on foot, passing the brightly lit houses without stopping. He thought about letting them know she was alone and that it might be a good idea to send someone to check on her, but he couldn't talk to anyone just then. Maybe he'd call someone from his cabin; they'd swapped phone numbers earlier during the search for Shelby.

He paused in the deep shadows by the private drive sign. This, he thought, was where Landon had grabbed her. Where Maggie had found Shelby's phone. She must have been so frightened. So close to home, yet so far from safety. Had she thought of him, wished she had allowed him to walk her home as he had offered? She'd said she didn't blame him for not being with her then.

She had every right to blame him for walking out on her now.

He turned, looked back at the lights glowing in the Bell family compound. Living so close together, working together, eating together—and yet Shelby was alone tonight. By choice. She hadn't asked any of them to stay with her.

She had asked him.

He'd have thought by now she'd have figured out he wasn't the type to stay around. He couldn't even stay in one job without getting bored. Not that he could imagine ever getting bored with Shelby. Just the opposite, in fact—he hadn't stopped going full-tilt since she'd hug-attacked him at the gas station. He'd been fascinated, amused, confused, terrified, hot and bothered—but he'd never once been bored.

And he was walking away from her.

He could almost hear his brother's voice in his ears. *Idiot.*

He looked toward Shelby's trailer, then over his shoulder toward Cabin Eight. *It's time to make a decision, bro.*

"I'm trying, Andrew," he muttered aloud, his voice a hollow echo in the darkness. "I'm trying."

Shelby was still sitting on the couch fifteen minutes after Aaron left, trying to get up the energy to put on pajamas and crawl into bed. She was so tired she thought she'd fall asleep immediately. She only hoped she wouldn't dream about waking up bound and gagged in Cabin Seven.

When someone tapped lightly on her door, she assumed it was a member of her family checking on her. Probably Maggie. Maybe Lori. Maybe she needed a couple hours of girl talk and commiseration from someone who'd understand the ramifications of getting involved with Mr. Heartache-in-the-Making, something both Maggie and Lori would understand all too well.

She opened the door with her good hand, then froze when she saw who stood on the porch. "Did you forget something?"

Aaron nodded sheepishly. "I forgot to tell you I'm a coward and an idiot. I'm sure Andrew would be happy to confirm both those things if you call him, but I'm hoping you won't."

Her heart fluttering crazily now, she cocked her head. "You are not a coward," she said flatly. "Not after the way you rescued me earlier. You are, however, an idiot."

For some reason, that made him laugh. "Yes. May I come back in?"

"That depends. Are you here to tell me goodbye again? Because, you know—been there, done that."

"Actually, I thought I might hang around awhile," he said after taking a deep breath. "Steven's going to be out of commission for a few more weeks, and your uncle Bryan needs more help than a few high school kids. What I said about the job being great for someone who likes being outdoors? Who enjoys being around people? Who hates being tied to a desk from nine to five? I've just realized that maybe I was talking about myself."

For the first time she realized that hope could hurt almost as much as heartache. In a different way, perhaps, but both could end in disappointment. "You want to try resort management for your new career?"

"It certainly has its appeal," he said, his voice deepening as he took another step forward.

She moved backward to allow him inside, slowly closing the door. "I thought you didn't want to be surrounded by family. Didn't want to work in a family business."

He shrugged. "I don't want to work in *my* family business," he corrected her. "I love them all, but doing computer searches and stakeouts and endless meetings bores me senseless. Do you think there's an opening for me here?"

"I'm sure we could work something out," she whispered. "You really want to stay and work here?"

"I want to stay with you," he corrected. "I've liked what I've seen of the work, but I'm more interested in seeing what happens between us. Maybe it's happened fast, but I think what we have is special, Shelby. So special it almost scared me into taking to my heels. Almost losing you this morning—well, that made me realize exactly how much you've come to mean to me. And tonight it all sort of crashed on top of me and I freaked out."

Which was what she'd seen when she'd looked at him, she thought. "I think we've found something special, too, Aaron. And I couldn't bear the thought of just saying goodbye and maybe never seeing you again. But you don't have to work for the family just for my sake. We can see each other when we can, talk on the phone every day—"

He shook his head. "If you think your family would approve, I'd like to try it, at least for the summer. I've been comfortable here from the first day, fascinated by all that goes into running the place."

"Then maybe, if you decide resort management doesn't interest you, we'll look around for something that appeals to us both," she suggested, feeling uncharacteristically shy as she tucked a curl behind her right ear.

Moving closer to her, Aaron cupped her face in his hands, his fingers achingly gentle against her bruised skin. "You're saying you could be willing to leave this place you love so much for me?"

Wrapping her arms around his waist, she smiled mistily up at him. "If things work out between us the way I think they will, I would most definitely be open to negotiation. I know I'll always be welcome here, to stay or to visit, but like Steven, ultimately I need to follow my heart."

Taking care with her bruised lips, he kissed her tenderly. "We'll worry about the details later," he promised. "Right now, I want to tuck you into bed and just hold you all night. Just to assure myself that you're safe and you're here with me."

Nestling her cheek against his shoulder, she released a deep breath. "I like the sound of that."

He wrapped an arm around her shoulders. "Maybe you'd like to show me your bedroom?"

"Absolutely."

Though she was still convinced she could have managed on her own, it was nice to have Aaron's help donning her pajamas with her sore wrist and brushing her hair over her stitches. She could tell he was still struggling with guilt about what had happened to her, but that would fade with time. Maybe not quite as quickly as her bruises, but she would do her best to convince him that he was blameless in the attack.

Her bed was smaller than the queen-size in the cabin, but he didn't complain when they lay curled together, her head nestled on his chest. "This is nice," she said, her injured wrist resting lightly against him.

"I could get used to it pretty fast," he admitted with a chuckle. He was starting to sound like himself again, easy and cheery. She was glad.

"Shelby?"

Her eyes were already closed, her mind drifting. "Mmm?"

"Is it too soon for me to tell you that I think I fell in love with you the minute you threw yourself at me at the gas station?"

Her pulse tripped a little, but she kept her tone casual when she replied, "It took me a little longer. I fell in love over iced tea and a cherry freeze inside the station— when you didn't make fun of me for thinking you were

Andrew and asking you to investigate one of our guests. I thought, finally—here's someone who really gets me."

His lips brushed her forehead. "It's happened pretty fast between us. But my family has a history of that. A very successful history, as it turns out."

Smiling, she said, "We wouldn't want to spoil that good record."

"I don't think there's any danger of that."

Letting her eyes close again, she murmured, "Neither do I. I have a very good feeling about this. And so far my instincts have turned out to be pretty reliable."

"You've made a believer out of me," he assured her.

She was still smiling when she drifted into sleep, safe in Aaron's arms.

Shelby had informed Aaron that the Bell family gathered for a breakfast meeting every Monday morning at six in the grill, before opening the marina, store and office. They discussed the upcoming week's projects, informally reported on the state of their own responsibilities, discussed ideas and expenses. These Monday meetings had been started by Pop and his sons years ago, before she was even born, when their once-small marina and campground had started evolving into the thriving resort of today.

Shelby admitted she had loved accompanying her parents to the meetings as a child, having breakfast at one of the diner tables and listening to the discussions about the state of the resort. She'd begun to participate with ideas and suggestions—some admittedly far-fetched—by the time she was a young teen. Now it was her job to present financial reports every Monday morning, a responsibility she took very seriously.

She had another order of business this particular

Monday morning. Aaron followed her past the closed sign at twenty minutes past six. They'd have been earlier, but when they had awakened this morning in each other's arms, their whispers of love still echoing in the room, they'd had to celebrate being together. Aaron had tried to be very careful of Shelby's injuries, but she'd been impatient with his restraint, flipping him onto his back and demonstrating just how resilient she was.

He would have been perfectly content to stay right there in her bed all day, but she'd urged him to attend the meeting with her. For one thing, she wanted to reassure everyone that she was okay, she'd said. She hadn't missed a Monday-morning meeting in years, and they would assume if she didn't show up this time that she was too incapacitated by trauma, which piqued her pride.

Everyone else was gathered there when they entered the diner, even Lori and Steven, who had a pair of crutches propped beside him. Shelby had told Aaron to expect to see everyone but Lori, who didn't usually attend the meetings, even when she was home from college and working in the office, but there she was, sitting between her grandparents. Aaron figured her presence this morning was an indication of how harrowing yesterday's events had been. As seemed usual in times of stress, this family had drawn closer together, other issues temporarily set aside.

Shelby was welcomed into the room with loving smiles, relief obvious on every face that she was there with them, a little battered but otherwise in one piece. Aaron imagined Steven had been greeted in much the same way.

Her mother hurried to her side and kissed her bruised cheek. "How do you feel, honey?"

"I'm fine, Mom. The wrist is still a little sore, but no headache."

"Good." Smiling at Aaron, Sarah said, "Sit down, I'll get your breakfast. We're having waffles, fruit and bacon this morning."

"Sounds good, Mom," Shelby said, "but first I need to tell you all something."

Considering her tendency to drift into stream-of-consciousness chatter when she was enthusiastic, there was no telling what Shelby would say next. Aaron found himself anticipating her announcement with a stifled grin, finding that aspect of her as appealing as all the other facets he'd discovered thus far. He looked forward to learning even more about her in coming weeks—years, he amended with a rush of slightly nervous anticipation.

All heads had turned their way, everyone quiet as they waited for Shelby to speak again. A few questioning sideways glances were directed at him, as if they wondered how he was involved with this big announcement.

"My plan for this morning was to tell you all that Aaron's time with us is ending," Shelby said. "I was going to explain that he and I have been seeing each other, but I've decided it's not going anywhere, so I've chosen to end it."

Thoroughly amused, Aaron noted her family looked bewildered as they glanced from Shelby to him to each other.

"You're, um, breaking up with him?" her brother asked with a frown. With some satisfaction, Aaron thought he saw a hint of disappointment in Steven's expression. Nice to know he'd made at least one good friend in Shelby's family.

"That was the plan," Shelby agreed cheerfully. "I was going to send him away—dejected and bitterly disappointed, of course."

"Shelby—" her father said with a shake of his head.

She wrapped her right hand beneath Aaron's arm and grinned. "I've changed my mind, Dad. I've decided to keep him."

"What Shelby is trying to say," Aaron interjected when her family looked even more confused, "is that I'd like to stay around for a while. I know you need someone to fill in for Steven and I'd like to apply for that job. You can hire me on a probationary basis if you want, let us all see how it works out, but I can guarantee you I'll be a dedicated employee. I can supply references, if needed," he added with a crooked smile.

Pop cocked a bushy eyebrow. "From your twin brother, Andrew?"

Still unable to tell if the old guy was pulling his leg, Aaron smiled and agreed, "He would probably vouch for me in person, if it would help."

Maybe seeing him and Andrew side by side would finally convince Pop that there really were two of them—assuming he hadn't been joking about that all along.

"You want to work for the resort?" Sarah asked as if she needed clarification.

He nodded. "If you all agree."

Everyone glanced at Bryan. He shrugged. "The man's a hard worker. Good with a hammer. Experienced in construction work. Puts the family first. I say give him a shot."

C.J. didn't look as nonchalant. He scowled as he looked from Aaron to Shelby and back. "If you hurt my daughter—"

"Dad." Shelby spoke with more steel than Aaron had

heard from her before. "When it comes to the resort, you have a vote. My personal life is off-limits, remember?"

Aaron thought it had to take a massive effort, but C.J. subsided with a huff of breath. "Fine. We'll give him a chance."

Aaron decided he needed to have Shelby teach him how to deal with family that way.

Everyone started talking at once—about his and Shelby's plans, more rehashing of yesterday, the regular business discussed in the Monday-morning meetings—and then the room fell silent again when someone new entered.

Linda gasped and jumped from her chair to rush toward the doorway. "Hannah! We weren't expecting you back yet. What a nice surprise."

Two facts were immediately apparent to Aaron when he first laid eyes on Shelby's cousin Hannah. One, she was gorgeous. Stunning, actually. And two, she was pregnant. He'd estimate about six months along. Quickly putting together a few of the things the others had said about her, he realized he should have already figured that out.

"How did you get here so early?" Linda asked, leading Hannah in. "You must have left Mother's house before dawn."

"I did," Hannah admitted. "I couldn't sleep, anyway, and I wanted to get ahead of the traffic. I'll rest this afternoon. I was just ready to be home."

"So much has happened in the short time you've been away," Linda said with a breathless laugh. "We'll have to tell you all about it. First, say hello to—"

Hannah gasped loudly, her face draining of color. Staring at Aaron, she swayed visibly.

He was close enough to reach her before she could

fall, supporting her on one side while her mother caught her other arm. The family jumped up, hurrying toward her, but Shelby waved them back, urging them to give Hannah some air.

Steadying herself, dark-haired Hannah stared up at Aaron with shocked green eyes. "Andrew," she whispered. "I—"

And then she stopped, a frown creasing her eyebrows. "Wait. You're not—"

"I'm Aaron," he said gently. "Andrew's twin."

She drew a deep, unsteady breath. "You're Aaron."

"Yes." Unlike the others, she didn't seem surprised that Andrew had a twin, though seeing him had certainly shaken her.

Aaron looked down at her swollen belly, doing some quick mental calculations. No. It had been ten months since Andrew was here at the resort. If he'd seen Hannah since, no one had mentioned it—and knowing this family, they would have mentioned it.

"I'm sorry," she said. "It was a long drive and I'm operating on little sleep."

"I'm sure seeing Aaron and thinking he was Andrew brought back a lot of unhappy memories," her mother sympathized. "But Aaron's presence here has nothing to do with Wade or any of that unpleasantness last year, Hannah. Actually, he's going to be staying for a while, working with your dad."

"Oh. Well, that's—" Hannah swallowed audibly. "That's nice. I need to sit down."

While the others all gathered around Hannah, helping her to a chair, fetching water and food for her, asking questions and talking about all she had missed, Shelby slipped her hand beneath Aaron's arm again with a soft laugh. "If it's not one drama, it's another in this family. Maybe you'd like to run while you can?"

His attention focused on her pretty smile, he had to bend his head for a quick kiss, regardless of how many members of her family were in the room. "Too late. I think I'm hooked."

"Well, don't expect me to throw you back." She leaned against him, smiling happily. "I caught you, I'm keeping you."

Kissing her again, more slowly this time, he decided he had no problem with that. He'd been looking a long time for his place in the world. He'd always believed he would know when he found it.

He knew now. He was home. With Shelby. And this adventure was going to last a lifetime.

* * * * *

COMING NEXT MONTH
from Harlequin® Special Edition®
AVAILABLE MARCH 19, 2013

#2251 HER HIGHNESS AND THE BODYGUARD

The Bravo Royales

Christine Rimmer

Princess Rhiannon Bravo-Calabretti has loved only one man in her life—orphan turned soldier Captain Marcus Desmarais—but he walked away knowing that she deserved more than a commoner. Years later, fate stranded them together overnight in a freak spring blizzard...and gave them an unexpected gift!

#2252 TEN YEARS LATER...

Matchmaking Mamas

Marie Ferrarella

Living in Tokyo, teaching English, Sebastian Hunter flees home to his suddenly sick mother's side just in time to attend his high school reunion. Brianna MacKenzie, his first love, looks even better than she had a decade ago...but can he win her over for the second and final time?

#2253 MARRY ME, MENDOZA

The Fortunes of Texas: Southern Invasion

Judy Duarte

Because of a stipulation in her employment contract, Nicole Castleton needs to marry before she can become the CEO of Castleton Boots. Her plan to reunite with ex-high school sweetheart Miguel Mendoza was strictly business—until their hearts got in the way!

#2254 A BABY IN THE BARGAIN

The Camdens of Colorado

Victoria Pade

After what her great-grandfather did to his family, bitter Gideon Thatcher refuses to hear a word of January Camden's apology...or get close to the beautiful brunette. Plus, she's desperate to have a baby, and Gideon does *not* see children in his future. But after spending time together, they may find they share more than just common ground....

#2255 THE DOCTOR AND MR. RIGHT

Rx for Love

Cindy Kirk

Dr. Michelle Kerns has a "no kids" rule when it comes to dating men...until she meets her hunky neighbor who has a child—a thirteen-year-old girl to be exact! Her mind says no, but maybe this one rule *is* meant to be broken!

#2256 THE TEXAN'S FUTURE BRIDE

Byrds of a Feather

Sheri WhiteFeather

Suffering from amnesia, J.D. wandered aimlessly through Buckshot Hills until Jenna Byrd offered the injured cowboy a place to stay. Slowly memories flood back to him, but what he remembers makes him want to run away from love—*fast*. Yet why can't he keep himself out of beautiful Jenna's embrace?

You can find more information on upcoming Harlequin® titles,
free excerpts and more at www.HarlequinInsideRomance.com.

HSECNM0313

REQUEST YOUR FREE BOOKS!

2 FREE NOVELS PLUS 2 FREE GIFTS!

⊕ HARLEQUIN®

SPECIAL EDITION

Life, Love & Family

YES! Please send me 2 FREE Harlequin® Special Edition novels and my 2 FREE gifts (gifts are worth about $10). After receiving them, if I don't wish to receive any more books, I can return the shipping statement marked "cancel." If I don't cancel, I will receive 6 brand-new novels every month and be billed just $4.49 per book in the U.S. or $5.24 per book in Canada. That's a savings of at least 14% off the cover price! It's quite a bargain! Shipping and handling is just 50¢ per book in the U.S. and 75¢ per book in Canada.* I understand that accepting the 2 free books and gifts places me under no obligation to buy anything. I can always return a shipment and cancel at any time. Even if I never buy another book, the two free books and gifts are mine to keep forever.

235/335 HDN FVTV

Name _____ (PLEASE PRINT)

Address _____ Apt. #

City _____ State/Prov. _____ Zip/Postal Code

Signature (if under 18, a parent or guardian must sign)

Mail to the Harlequin® Reader Service:
IN U.S.A.: P.O. Box 1867, Buffalo, NY 14240-1867
IN CANADA: P.O. Box 609, Fort Erie, Ontario L2A 5X3

Want to try two free books from another line?
Call 1-800-873-8635 or visit www.ReaderService.com.

* Terms and prices subject to change without notice. Prices do not include applicable taxes. Sales tax applicable in N.Y. Canadian residents will be charged applicable taxes. Offer not valid in Quebec. This offer is limited to one order per household. Not valid for current subscribers to Harlequin Special Edition books. All orders subject to credit approval. Credit or debit balances in a customer's account(s) may be offset by any other outstanding balance owed by or to the customer. Please allow 4 to 6 weeks for delivery. Offer available while quantities last.

Your Privacy—The Harlequin® Reader Service is committed to protecting your privacy. Our Privacy Policy is available online at www.ReaderService.com or upon request from the Harlequin Reader Service.

We make a portion of our mailing list available to reputable third parties that offer products we believe may interest you. If you prefer that we not exchange your name with third parties, or if you wish to clarify or modify your communication preferences, please visit us at www.ReaderService.com/consumerchoice or write to us at Harlequin Reader Service Preference Service, P.O. Box 9062, Buffalo, NY 14269. Include your complete name and address.

HSE13

***

How could this have happened?

Rhiannon Bravo-Calabretti, Princess of Montedoro, could not believe it. Honestly. What were the odds?

One in ten, maybe? One in twenty? She supposed that it could have been just the luck of the draw. After all, her country was a small one and there were only so many rigorously trained bodyguards to be assigned to the members of the princely family.

However, when you added in the fact that Marcus Desmarais wanted nothing to do with her ever again, reasonable odds became pretty much no-way-no-how. Because he would have said no.

So why hadn't he?

A moment later she realized she knew why: because if he refused the assignment, his superiors might ask questions. Suspicion and curiosity could be roused, and he wouldn't have wanted that.

Stop.

Enough. Done. She was simply not going to think about it—about *him*—anymore.

She needed to focus on the spare beauty of this beautiful wedding in the small town of Elk Creek, Montana. Her sister was getting married. Everyone was seated in the little church.

Still, *he* would be standing. In back somewhere by the doors, silent and unobtrusive. Just like the other security people. Her shoulders ached from the tension, from the certainty he was watching her, those eerily level, oh-so-serious, almost-green eyes staring twin holes in the back of her head.

It doesn't matter. Forget about it, about him.

It didn't matter why he'd been assigned to her. He was there to protect her, period. And it was for only this one day and the evening. Tomorrow she would fly home again. And be free of him. Forever.

She could bear anything for a single day. It had been a shock, that was all. And now she was past it.

She would simply ignore him. How hard could that be?

***

Don't miss HER HIGHNESS AND THE BODYGUARD, coming in April 2013 in Harlequin® Special Edition®.

And look for Alice's story, HOW TO MARRY A PRINCESS, only from Harlequin® Special Edition®, in November 2013.

HARLEQUIN®

SPECIAL EDITION

Life, Love and Family

Looking for your next
Fortunes of Texas: Southern Invasion fix?

Coming next month
MARRY ME, MENDOZA
by Judy Duarte

Because of a stipulation in her employment
contract, Nicole Castleton needs to marry before
she can become the CEO of Castleton Boots.
Her plan to reunite with former high school
sweetheart Miguel Mendoza was strictly
business—until their hearts got in the way!

*Available in April 2013 from Harlequin Special Edition
wherever books are sold.*

There's magic—and love—in those Texas hills!

THE TEXAN'S FUTURE BRIDE
by Sheri WhiteFeather

Suffering from amnesia, J.D. wandered aimlessly through Buckshot Hills until Jenna Byrd offered the injured cowboy a place to stay. Slowly memories seep back to him, but what he remembers makes him want to run away from love—*fast*. Yet why can't he keep himself out of beautiful Jenna's embrace?

Look for the second title in the *Byrds of a Feather* miniseries next month!

Available in April 2013 from Harlequin Special Edition wherever books are sold.

www.Harlequin.com

HSE65738

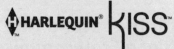